"What a revolting man you are!"

Jan stared at him. "And what a revolting view you have of human nature."

Marc's face hardened, his lips forming a thin, angry line. He stepped forward and Jan felt his hands on her shoulders. She could feel the fury vibrating through his fingers.

"You little vixen!" he growled between gritted teeth. "I'll remind you who happens to be in charge of this expedition. You're working for me, remember? All right, so you keep this room. But since it's so sumptuous, we'll use it for any discussions we need to have about the job, and I'll consider it my right to come in and out as I please.

"Except when you're in bed, of course," he added silkily. "I wouldn't dream of intruding then."

Nicola West, born on the south coast of England, now lives in central England with her husband and family. She always knew she wanted to write. She started writing articles on many subjects, a regular column in a county magazine, children's stories and women's magazine stories before tackling her first book. Though she had three novels published before she became a Harlequin author, she feels her first novel for Harlequin was a turning point in her career. Her settings are usually places that she has seen for herself.

Books by Nicola West

A WOMAN'S PLACE

Nicola West

Harlequin Books

TORONTO • NEW YORK • LONDON
AMSTERDAM • PARIS • SYDNEY • HAMBURG
STOCKHOLM • ATHENS • TOKYO • MILAN

Original hardcover edition published in 1990
by Mills & Boon Limited

ISBN 0-373-03101-7

Harlequin Romance first edition January 1991

CHAPTER ONE

'MARC TYRELL? You're seriously asking *me* to work on his next programme?' Janis Cartwright sat up straight in the low armchair and stared unbelievingly at the woman opposite her. 'Lucia, you know the kind of reputation he's got!'

Lucia Smiley, five feet nothing, plump and untidy with straggling grey hair, the face of an amiable aunt and a reputation of her own for producing some of the most off-beat programmes on television, grinned amiably and opened yet another packet of cigarettes. 'That's right, Jan. And you needn't wrinkle your nose up like that—I know you think smoking's a disgusting habit. So do I, as a matter of fact. So does Marc Tyrell, as it happens. You ought to think yourselves lucky you never started, the pair of you.'

Jan seized at once on the last four words. '*Pair* of us? That's something we're never likely to be. Lucia, you're not really thinking of putting us together, are you?'

'And why not?' With a sudden flash of the incisiveness that had got her to the position of top producer in 90s-TV, Lucia leant forward. 'All right, Jan, I know his reputation. One of the sharpest directors around and I'm damned lucky to have him in my stable. One of these days, he'll be sitting where I'm sitting now. And the way he's going on, it'll be sooner than I like! Yes, he's a difficult man to work for and with. Yes, he expects perfection, and yes, he does his best to provide it himself.

What's wrong with all that? Afraid you won't measure up to his standards?'

Jan flushed. Her topaz eyes showed momentary sparks of anger. 'Of course not!' She paused, aware that she had answered too quickly and that Lucia, who missed nothing, had noticed it. *Was* she subconsciously afraid of that? But that was nonsense—hadn't she had it dinned into her since early childhood that no man was necessarily better than a woman, that women could live their own lives, run their own careers, prove themselves equal in every way. . .?

'Just what do you have against working with Marc Tyrell?' Lucia asked softly, and Jan gave her an exasperated glance.

'Well, what do you think? It's his insufferable chauvinism, of course. I mean, you only have to look at him! The size of him, for a start—six foot three if he's an inch, dark, rugged—he's just impossibly good-looking *and* he knows it. He expects every woman he meets to fall adoringly at his feet, and he believes that's the right place for them. I don't suppose the idea of a woman with brains has ever entered his head.' She paused, thinking of the man she had never actually met, only seen around the building and heard of by repute. 'And it's not just that,' she added with some reluctance. 'It's the way he looks at me sometimes. . . We don't even know each other, except by sight, yet he makes me feel. . .' She stopped, aware of how ridiculous it was going to sound if she said, He makes me feel as if he can see everything that's going on in my mind. No. Lucia would think she had gone mad. And maybe she had. Wasn't working with Marc Tyrell just the job that any of the researchers at 90s-TV would give their right arms for? So why wasn't she jumping at it like a dog at a ball?

Lucia was watching her narrowly. She stubbed out her cigarette, half finished.

'Well, I never expected to hear Jan Cartwright talking like an adolescent,' she said briskly. 'I'd have expected you to have grown out of those sort of ideas years ago. So he's good-looking. Is that his fault? And if other women have to act foolish, does that mean you have to? Or that he even expects you to? Don't you think he might even be thankful to find a girl who *doesn't* swoon away at the sight of him? I imagine even constant adoration could get boring. As for not expecting women to have brains—well, you may be right. But if you are, I wonder you don't jump at the opportunity to prove him wrong. It's a chance for you, Jan, a chance in more ways than one.'

Jan gave her a rueful look. 'You're right, of course. I'm behaving like an idiot. Yes, I would like to prove him wrong—I would like to show him a woman who's impervious to his masculine charms.' Her eyes gleamed. 'It could even be fun. . . All right, I'll do it.' Her quick smile lit her eyes to flame. 'What's the assignment, anyway? Must be something interesting, or you'd never have put him on it.'

Lucia paused in the act of lighting her next cigarette. She glanced up through the smoke and for a second Jan was reminded sharply of a medieval witch, peering through the fumes of a simmering cauldron of spells. She felt her lips pull into another smile, this time of admiration and affection. To look at Lucia as she walked through the city streets to work of a morning, you might have thought she was the office cleaner. Yet once inside the building, she commanded more respect than any man in 90s-TV.

Except for one, Jan thought then. Marc Tyrell.

Recently come here from one of the big corporations, already stalking the corridors as if he owned them. As even Lucia appeared to expect him to do, and not so very far in the future, either.

A man, marching in and taking over what had been a woman's domain—and a very successful one at that. And Jan looked at Lucia, drawing now on her cigarette and filling the office with its acrid smell, and knew that, to her, 90s-TV and Lucia Smiley were both interchangeable and inseparable. And if anyone should be sitting in that chair, some time in the distant future, it shouldn't be any man. It should be a woman.

Preferably Janis Cartwright.

'Jan?' said Lucia, and she realised with a jerk that Lucia had been speaking. 'You with me? Did you hear what I said?'

Jan shook herself. 'I'm sorry, no—something else came into my mind. What was it, Lucia?'

'About the assignment,' Lucia repeated patiently, and Jan remembered her question. 'I think I'd rather leave it to Marc himself to tell you that. There'll be quite a lot of details to sort out. . .' She reached forward and shuffled vaguely among the papers on the low table between them, and Jan knew that the interview was at an end. 'You'll find him in now, I shouldn't wonder— why not pop along and have a word?'

Jan stood up, looking down at the short, plump figure with a mixture of affection and exasperation. Pop along and have a word, indeed! Did Lucia really suppose she didn't know that it was already set up—that Marc was waiting in his own office for her at this very moment, knowing she would have agreed to work with him, knowing that whatever argument she'd put up Lucia would have demolished it with ease? She felt a brief urge to rebel, to say that she wasn't prepared to do it after all, that she didn't like being manipulated. . . And then she thought of Marc Tyrell, who had already collected half a dozen awards for his programmes, who invariably shed glory like golden rain on all those who worked with him. She'd be crazy to pass up such a chance simply because of his reputation. And anyway, she could handle him, couldn't she? She'd never yet met the man who could get the better of her—and, as Lucia had pointed out, Marc Tyrell could prove a very enjoyable challenge. . .

'Yes, that's a good idea,' she said with a trace of irony in her voice which Lucia immediately noticed and appreciated with a grin of such wickedness that Jan couldn't help laughing. 'I'll pop along now. Perhaps he'll even have a pot of tea to share with me. And the best china, naturally.'

'But naturally,' Lucia agreed, her face perfectly straight now. 'Marc Tyrell is a man of impeccable taste and style, if nothing else.' She smiled again. 'Don't worry, Jan. He won't turn you into a "little woman" trotting eagerly three steps behind him. He does understand that women are equal to men. And even if he didn't, I can't think of anyone better than you to persuade him.'

'Does he?' Jan's voice was grim. 'That's not what I've heard. But you're right, Lucia, if he tries any male chauvinist stuff with me he'll have a surprise coming to him.' She smiled. 'Maybe I'm even looking forward to it. Are you sure you won't tell me just what we're going to be doing?'

Lucia shook her head firmly. 'Not a chance. He wants to tell you himself—to see your reaction, I'd guess. So get along there and satisfy your curiosity. I'll just tell you this—I think you'll enjoy it.'

'As the actress said to the bishop,' Jan remarked flippantly, and backed hastily to the door. 'All right, I'm going! And—Lucia——'

'Yes?'

'Thanks,' Jan said meekly, and escaped into the corridor.

Outside, she took a deep breath. So this was why Lucia had wanted her in early! Obviously there was something special on. It wasn't surprising that Marc Tyrell was part of it—but herself! She felt a quick glow of pleasure—the work she had put in during the year she'd been with 90s-TV had obviously borne fruit. But the glow was followed equally quickly by a chill of trepidation. Marc Tyrell was known for not suffering fools gladly—and, at the same time, for being something of a philanderer. Wasn't there some story of a girl at the last company he'd worked for, who'd ended up emigrating?

Well, he won't break *my* heart, Jan thought robustly. The man isn't alive who could do that. And she thanked her mother mentally, for having brought her up with such firm ideals and making her fit to cope with anything she might meet in a world that was still far too male-orientated.

As for not suffering fools gladly—well, she wasn't a fool, was she? Lucia clearly had confidence in her, and that ought to be enough for anyone. So really there wasn't a thing to worry about.

All the same—even though she knew that Lucia wouldn't have bothered, would have marched into Marc Tyrell's presence with her skirt (if she was wearing one instead of her usual trousers) drooping, and her jumper sagging—Jan slipped into the cloakroom and took a quick look at herself in the mirror to make sure that her linen suit was uncreased and her soft, red-brown curls as tidy as good cutting could make them.

There was nothing to be done about her freckles, of course. But at least it was only spring and the summer sun hadn't brought them out in all their glory; they were at present little more than a dusting of gold across her nose and cheeks. And there was nothing to be done about the extreme youthfulness of her sparkling eyes and dimpling grin. She would just have to keep a straight face and try to look twenty-four instead of the nineteen that so many people seemed to take her for.

Which wouldn't be hard, she thought, working with Marc Tyrell. From what she'd heard, anyone who worked with him automatically aged ten years.

Looking back on that interview later, Jan saw that all the warning signs had been there, unrecognised at the time. But she hadn't been looking for them then. Her armour firmly in place, on the look-out for the slightest sign of male chauvinism, she had been watching for other things.

It started off calmly enough. She and Marc had seen each other around, of course—in a company as small as 90s-TV it was difficult not to know everyone by sight, although, since crews tended to stick together once they had begun work on any particular programme, location work kept Marc out of the studios for most of the time. Location! For the first time, she wondered if they would be working outside much, and felt a thrill of excitement. Ever since she had begun working as a researcher in 90s-TV, she had loved location work. Going to new places, finding out about the people, the events, often turning up facts that had been hidden or overlooked—all this added sparkle to the job, and her very enjoyment of it caused her to excel. More than one director had commented that Jan's enthusiasm had brought an extra dimension to the programme. It would not be long, Lucia had said once, before she was directing herself—she just needed a little more experience, that was all.

The door to Marc Tyrell's office was ajar, and she knocked on it and then pushed it open. It was almost identical to Lucia's—large enough for a desk in one corner and a seating area, with a few low armchairs arranged around a coffee-table. But to Jan's surprise there were unexpected differences—Lucia's office was spartan, almost deviod of decoration or ornament, the coffee-table and desk smothered with piled papers, some of which had overflowed on to the floor. If you were offered coffee by Lucia it came out of the vending machine, in plastic beakers, and the only other accessory was a huge ashtray, heaped with cigarette ends.

Marc Tyrell's office, in contrast, was immaculately tidy and definitely masculine—but on the corner of the desk there was a bronze sculpture of a horse's head, on the coffee-table stood a tray which did indeed bear a coffee-pot and real china mugs, and standing on the window-sill was a carved wooden animal—an otter, Jan thought, its front paws resting on a rock, eyes alert. She could almost see its whiskers quivering.

Lucia might have been joking about Marc Tyrell having taste and style, but she was certainly right. And for some reason Jan found that disconcerting. It turned her preconceived notions about him upside-down.

Hastily she pulled herself together. A man could have the most discerning taste and still be difficult. China mugs, bronzes and a carved otter meant nothing. She looked at the man who was working at the desk and met his eyes.

Steel-grey eyes. The eyes that had already made her feel he could see straight into her mind. Eyes that glimmered under dark brows, eyes that could penetrate like a surgeon's scalpel; eyes that revealed the kind of man Marc Tyrell was.

'Good morning,' she said before he could speak. 'I'm Jan Cartwright. I understand I'm to work with you on your next documentary.'

'Ah, Jan, yes. Come in—have some coffee.' His voice was deep and pleasant and he got up at once, his smile showing the white, even teeth that film stars spent hours in a dentist's chair to achieve. In here, he looked even taller than Jan had thought him, and to her annoyance she had to tilt her head back to look up at him—a concession that, at five feet nine, she didn't have to make to many men.

Marc indicated a chair and Jan sat down in it, conscious that her cream linen skirt was revealing quite a length of leg. She could see that Marc had noticed it too, and her annoyance increased. Why did this kind of thing have to creep into every man-woman relationship, even when it was strictly a business one? Gritting her teeth a little, she waited for him to make some fatuous remark about how pleasant it would be to work with such a delightful companion—following it up, no doubt, with the implication that, delightful companions being invariably brainless, *he* would be having to do most of the work.

However, he said no such thing. Having poured the coffee, he settled himself in the opposite armchair and regarded her thoughtfully without speaking. Jan sat on, unmoving—he needn't think he was going to needle *her* into breaking the silence! After a moment or two she reached forward for her coffee and sipped it reflectively, then glanced up to find him still watching her.

'So what exactly is this assignment?' she asked before she could stop herself, and mentally kicked herself at the sight of Marc's twitching lips. Round one to him!

'Quite an interesting one, I think,' he said, and she felt the deep tones of his voice throb through the air. 'I hope you'll think so too—but of course, if you don't I'll expect you to say so at once. I can't work with anyone who isn't as enthusiastic as I am about the subject.'

'Naturally not,' Jan said stiffly. 'Any more than I would want to work on a project that didn't interest me.'

'Quite.' The grey eyes examined her again. 'Obviously we agree on that point, at least.' She had an uncomfortable feeling that somehow he'd scored again. 'Right, let's waste no more time.' He leaned forward and she saw the light in his eyes as he began to speak. 'We're calling this project—for the time being, anyway—*The Trail of the Great Detectives*. There's an increased interest in crime fiction these days, or maybe you don't take any notice of that kind of thing. And it's changing. Today's breed of crime writers—people like Rendell, P. D. James, Allbeury—they're giving us something new. Crime *novels*—books that tell us more than simply whodunnit and how. They're going into *why*—what makes a man, often an apparently ordinary, decent man, a criminal. What sends him over the top. How tiny incidents can lead to disaster. How a misunderstanding can lead to murder. Patricia Highsmith started it, of course, in America, but we're now producing some fine crime novelists of our own——' He broke off and the steel-grey eyes came to Jan's face, narrow and piercing. 'Well, how do you feel so far? Interested?'

'Yes, I am.' She spoke positively. 'Crime is my

favourite reading. I think it would be fascinating to explore the present trends. But surely you'll look at the past as well?'

'Certainly we will. We'll look at the lot. Conan Doyle—Christie—Sayers—we'll examine them all. Especially with relation to their running characters—Holmes, Poirot, Wimsey. We'll visit the places they used to set thir scenes, add a bit of drama with film clips where they exist, or newly written scenes. That's where you'll come in, of course—researching and setting up. It'll be quite a task.'

'Yes, I can see it will.' Jan caught his enthusiasm. Already she could visualise the settings. Dartmoor, with Holmes and Watson investigating the Hound of the Baskervilles. The Orient Express, with Poirot questioning each passenger in turn. There would be plenty of film available for those, of course, if permission was given to use it. But for others, new scripts would be needed, actors found. . . 'The Reichenbach Falls,' she said, thinking aloud. 'We ought to show the fight between Holmes and Moriarty, when Conan Doyle tried to kill him off. Isn't there a Sherlock Holmes Society which goes there and re-enacts it every year? We could film that. . . And Bond—James Bond! Does he count as a detective? We could show the settings as they are—as the author saw them—and compare them with the way they appear in the story or the film. There was a Bond film made in Switzerland. . .*On Her Majesty's Secret Service*. How long is the programme going to be? There's going to be an awful lot to fit in.'

Marc laughed. 'I can see you're as excited as I am! Well, all to the good. We should work well together. But let's get a few other points sorted out before we start to make plans. First of all, in answer to your question, the situation's fluid at the moment. If we can come up with a good enough scenario, we could run to several episodes, dealing with one or two writers and their characters a week. If not, we may have to squeeze it all into one half-hour to be kept as a spare, to fill in the gap between two big films on a holiday weekend.' But his tone and the look in his eye told Jan that he was unlikely to settle for as little as that. 'So you can see I want to be pretty sure that I pick the right team. And my researcher's going to be an important part of that team—we'll be working closely together and I can't afford to have any friction.' He looked squarely into her face and Jan bit her lip, remembering her words to Lucia. 'We've both got to be absolutely clear on this point.'

Did he mean that he was looking for a yes-man? Well, much as she wanted to work on this project, Jan wasn't going to make any promises of *that* kind! Lifting her chin a little, she met his eye and held it with her own.

'I hope I'm professional enough to be able to do my job without *friction*,' she said coolly. 'Although I won't give way on a point where I believe I'm right. Not unless you can convince me otherwise.'

'Even though I'll be the boss?' he asked, and she shivered at the thread of steel that seemed to run through his voice.

'Naturally you'll always have the last word.' And, looking at Marc Tyrell, she mentally added, *in more ways than one*. 'In such a case, I'd simply register my own views. But I've never had any complaints yet about my professional performance.'

There was a short silence. Again, his glance seemed to pierce deep into her mind, probing all the hidden recesses, all the dark and private places. He was trying to intimidate her, she thought angrily, trying to cow her into submission. Tightening her lips, she held the look and saw something pass across his face—some expression she couldn't identify, gone as quickly as it had appeared.

'Then that's agreed,' he said at last, smoothly. 'We work together purely as professionals. All right?'

'Is there any other way?' Jan asked coolly, and he grinned, looking suddenly younger.

'There could be—but we won't go into that now. Now—these other points I want to cover. . .' He began to talk, outlining his plans and telling her what would be expected of her. Jan listened, nodding occasionally. He certainly knew what he was doing. It was no wonder that his programmes were always of such excellent quality. She felt her enthusiasm rise again and she began to interject ideas of her own, suggesting slightly different angles, scenes that could be used in conjunction with each other to make a point, readings which could be used as voice-overs to illustrate landscape or scenery that had played an important part. . . She was startled when Marc glanced at his watch, gave an exclamation and rose to his feet.

'I've kept you here for two hours! I hope you hadn't any other appointments. . . Look, how about a spot of lunch? We can go on talking then—there still seems to be a lot to cover.'

Jan looked at him. He stood several inches taller than she and, in his dark suit, looked large, looming. . .almost threatening. For a moment, time seemed to shift slightly and she imagined herself standing with this man in some foreign place, strange and menacing. . .unsure as to whether the menace came from him or from something outside. . .something that enveloped them both, something that struck deep into her soul. . . Suddenly cold, she moved away a little and time came back once more into focus and he was Marc Tyrell, director of television programmes, and the only threat he presented was that of being a man.

And she could deal with that one. Hadn't she done so before, many, many times?

'Lunch?' she said coolly. 'No, I don't think I can make that, thank you. Perhaps we can arrange another meeting and carry on with our discussion then—that's if you do decide you want me in your team.'

'Of course,' he assented gravely enough, though she suspected there was a laugh somewhere in those grey eyes. 'Yes, let's do that. Let's see—when can we both make it?' He produced his diary. 'Day after tomorrow suit you? About two-thirty?'

'Yes, that's all right.' Jan opened her personal file and flipped through its pages. 'I've nothing on then.' She flicked him a quick glance, daring him to pick up her *faux pas* with some innuendo, but his face remained perfectly serious. 'Here? I'll see you then. And meanwhile I'll think of some more ideas for the programme.'

'Fine.' He moved to open the door for her, then stood back, leaving her to do it for herself. 'Sorry—I don't want to offend you with such old-world chivalry. Or have I read you wrong?'

'Read me wrong?'

'You're a feminist, aren't you? Into equality and all that? Woman in a man's world, making her own way, carving out a career, opening her own doors?' His voice was still serious, but Jan glanced at him with suspicion, certain that he was mocking her.

'And what if I am? Would you rather have a fluffy-headed little dolly-bird as a researcher? Someone with romance and marriage more on her mind than doing a good job? Someone who'd look up at you with big blue eyes and breathe adoration at you—"Yes, Mr Tyrell, no, Mr Tyrell, three bags full, Mr Tyrell." Because if you would——' Her tone betrayed her derision for those of her sex who filled this description, and Marc laughed.

'Heaven forbid! No, I'd much rather have a real woman, aware of her own worth and doing the job in her own way—bringing femininity to it as a balance, so that between us we present a true, rounded picture.' He looked at her thoughtfully. 'I admit I was brought up to open doors—but if you think that demeans you in some way, I'll be happy to let you open your own. But I won't be happy if you let your ideals get in the way of the work. Be very clear on that point, Jan.' His tone had hardened just enough to let her know that he meant it. 'I'll see you on Thursday—unless you change your mind. And I'll be glad to hear any fresh ideas you may have between now and then.'

He turned his back on her and walked to the window, leaving Jan standing irresolute a yard away from the door. Feeling decidedly uncomfortable, she hesitated, glancing at the broad back; but Marc didn't move and after a moment, knowing that he'd dismissed her and knowing too that she'd asked for the manner of her dismissal, she walked to the door and let herself out.

As she drew the door to after her, she paused and glanced back again. But Marc Tyrell hadn't moved. He was still standing at the window, his back to the room, apparently staring down into the street outside. His fingers were running lightly over the curved, sinuous back of the carved wooden otter.

CHAPTER TWO

'MARC TYRELL,' Jan's mother said thoughtfully. 'Well, he's certainly a good director—I've seen several of his programmes, although of course I've never worked with him. But is he really likely to take you as his researcher, Jan? I've heard he's not too keen on women colleagues—especially ones who aren't prepared to knuckle under to his every suggestion.'

'Just the impression I'd got,' Jan agreed. 'A real MCP. And I thought we'd strike sparks off each other right away. But somehow. . .'

'Don't tell me he charmed you!' Susan Cartwright gave her daughter a humorous glance. 'I thought better of you, Janis.'

Jan laughed. 'No, not quite. Although he certainly *could* switch on the charm if he wanted to. But I think I made my conditions quite clear—no sexism. And no patronisation. I'm to be there solely as a colleague and treated——'

'As another man?'

'As a *person*,' Jan said firmly, and her mother smiled approval.

'Well, if he accepts that it should be quite a feather in your cap. Marc Tyrell's appeared in the gossip columns quite a few times—seems that every female he meets falls at his feet. Finding one who doesn't could be quite a shock for the poor man. Not that I have any sympathy for him, of course. Men have had everything their own way for far too long.'

At that moment, Jan's father came out of his study. Tall, thin, with spectacles and a mild manner, he was a Professor of History at the local university. Most of his time was spent either in lectures or in writing learned volumes of historical biography, dealing mostly with long-dead figures that few people had ever heard of. He had met and married Jan's mother when she had become one of his students and since then had retired into a life that consisted almost entirely of his lecture-room and his study, emerging only to accompany his wife on such occasions as he could not avoid—when she collected her award for Best Newspaper Columnist, for instance, or when she was nominated for a presentation for Services to Women.

Jan remembered with amusement his efforts to get out of that one. 'They won't want a *husband* tagging along to that,' he'd protested, but Susan had been firm.

'Of course you must come. You're proof that feminists aren't totally devoid of normal emotion. Seeing me with a husband will stop any wagging tongues in their tracks.'

'If tongues have tracks,' Jan had said quietly, and her father had turned quickly.

'Take Janis, then. Isn't a daughter as good as a husband?'

'Certainly Janis will come too,' Susan had said. 'She'll be able to give you moral support. I want you both there.' And when she spoke in that tone, Professor Cartwright invariably subsided. They had all attended the presentation lunch.

Jan wondered occasionally just how often her mother had been forced to use that tone during the early days of their marriage. It was seldom enough now, for her father seemed to have evolved his own pattern of life, retreating into his study, taking just enough interest in his wife's activities to keep him out of trouble and burying himself in his own work. But what had he been like as a young man?

Dimly, she could remember him playing with her when she was a baby, reading to her as she sat on his knee, touching her hair with tender fingers as she drifted into sleep. But most of her childhood memories were of her mother—choosing her clothes, introducing her to books, bringing home toys that were 'educational' with which they played together, and always talking to her. Talking about the lives women had led in the past, the lives they could lead now in the future. 'They used to send women down the mines, to drag trucks of coal through underground passages,' Jan remembered her saying once. 'We don't do that now—women aren't even *allowed* down mines. But the point of equality is that we *should* be able to do it if we *want* to. And until that day comes women can never feel themselves truly equal.'

That was the message behind almost every word she wrote, both in her regular column and her articles, and in every word she spoke on radio or television. And she had done her best to make sure that her daughter believed and lived by every principle she had evolved.

All the same, much as she admired her mother, Jan had been conscious lately of faint stirrings of unease. She had to agree—what intelligent woman wouldn't?—that equality was a great ideal, to be worked, even fought, for. But had her mother really achieved it in her own life? With a husband who was already amiable to a fault, loving enough to grant her her own way in almost every whim, couldn't she have enjoyed equality of a different nature? Jan saw her father more and more as an isolated man, retreating to his own company at every opportunity, emerging only when forced. Wasn't that, she wondered—and felt disloyal even as she wondered it—wasn't that really more like domination?

Nevertheless, Jan had a deep affection for her father. There was a closeness between them which she did not feel with her mother. Looking at him now, standing at his study door with the paper in his hand, peering vaguely over the top of his spectacles, she felt a rush of love for him and went forward to kiss his cheek.

'Daddy, I'm going to work with Marc Tyrell on his new project. And guess what it's going to be about? All the great detectives!'

'Fictional detectives?' Susan Cartwright said quickly, before her husband could respond, and Jan nodded.

'That's right—Holmes, Poirot, Wimsey—all of them. We're going to research into each one and analyse what the author was doing, illustrating it with film clips or drama in the real setting the author had in mind. I thought I'd suggest you as chief consultant and adviser, Daddy!'

'A job he'd be well fitted for, considering the amount of detective fiction he gets through,' Susan said acidly. Reading detective fiction was Professor Cartwright's one relaxation and one of which she deeply disapproved; any light reading was anathema to her and she had been so eloquently critical of romantic novels that Jan had never even opened one. 'I'm surprised at Marc Tyrell, choosing to waste his time on a project like that.'

'He thinks that as they entertain a lot of people they're worth taking seriously,' Jan said mildly. 'And I agree with him. Anyway, we'll get to see a lot of interesting places—I'm hoping to persuade him to go to Switzerland for one episode.'

'Marc Tyrell?' Professor Cartwright asked, getting a word in at last. 'I know him——'

'I doubt that,' Susan said dismissively. 'He's a director, not a performer—although he does do his own interviewing, so I suppose it's possible. . . Anyway, Jan, the important thing is not to let him browbeat you. Look on it as an opportunity to make him see how good you are—how good women *can* be. Our sex has so much to give the world——'

'And I'll make sure everyone knows that,' Jan promised. 'One day, don't forget, I intend to be a director myself, and then I'll be able to make the kind of programmes *I* like. Until then, I just have to take all the opportunities that are offered and climb the ladder one rung at a time.'

'Well, it won't be long before you're at the top, whatever ladder you choose,' said Professor Cartwright, smiling at his daughter. 'Just don't be too hard on this poor fellow—did you say Tyrell? I wonder if that's——'

'Yes, Daddy. Marc Tyrell. He's very well known. And don't waste your sympathy on him—he's very well able to take care of himself.' Jan grinned at the thought of anyone being 'too hard' on Marc Tyrell, then added determinedly, 'And so am I. He needn't think he'll browbeat *me*—or have me grovelling at his feet! No, I'm looking forward to quite an interesting time. *Quite* an interesting time. . .'

It seemed, when they met again the following afternoon, that Marc Tyrell too was expecting great things of their partnership. No more was said about Jan being 'considered' for the job—as soon as she arrived, to find him clearing away the remains of a working lunch with another colleague, they went straight into the work. Marc had roughed out several ideas for the series and

Jan had spent the past two days jotting down her own thoughts. She explained them to Marc, who listened attentively.

'Well, we agreed the other day that the Reichenbach Falls are a must,' he said when she finished. 'But the restaurant on the top of the Schilthorn—I hadn't thought of that one.'

'It would be crazy to leave it out,' Jan urged. 'It's less than half a day's journey from Meiringen, where the falls are, and it was featured so well in *On Her Majesty's Secret Service*. From Sherlock Holmes to James Bond—you couldn't have a more striking contrast. And the setting's fabulous—the big revolving restaurant, set right on the peak of the mountain, almost three thousand metres above sea-level.' Her eyes glowed. 'If we could use a clip from the film and compare it with what the restaurant is actually like——'

'And what *is* it like? I take it you've been there.'

'I went there on holiday a couple of years ago. Oh, it's quite different from the film version—it was a luxurious mountain hide-away, wasn't it, full of beautiful girls. Typically Bond-ish.' Her voice made no secret of her feelings about that. 'But the restaurant itself is rather pleasant—nicely furnished, not overdone, good food and those fabulous views, wheeling slowly past. It's quite unbelievable.'

'Well, you obviously enjoyed it,' Marc said drily. 'All right, I'm convinced—we'll use it in the Bond sequence. Saves having to trek all the way to Bermuda! And maybe your idea of contrasting him with Holmes is a good one too. We might follow it through in the other episodes— taking, say, Lord Peter Wimsey and Adam Dalgliesh, or Hercule Poirot and Chief Inspector Wexford. Characters that have certain traits in common, yet make a sharp contrast. Mmm—we'll give that some more thought.'

Jan sat back, feeling absurdly pleased at having made an impression on this man, reputed to be a difficult director who demanded the best from everyone, including himself. Well, she could respect that—provided he respected her in turn.

She took the opportunity, as he sat poring over the papers that lay scattered on the table, to study him. Dark hair, grey eyes and a tall, muscular body all added up to conventional good looks. But Marc Tyrell had that extra something that prevented him from becoming just another hunk. A slight irregularity in his features, a cragginess that just saved his profile from perfection; a crookedness in his smile that lent it an attractiveness it would not have had if it had been too even, a slightly overlapping front tooth that proved he had never received the attentions of a cosmetic dentist.

She looked at his hands, moving over the papers. Long hands that looked as if they would be capable of any task from building a wall to conducting an orchestra, with long, tapering fingers sensitive enough to play a piano concerto. She wondered if he did, in fact, play any musical instrument.

And through it all, emanating from him as if it were some kind of unique force, was a vibrating energy, a throbbing urgency that ran through everything he did, so that anyone involved with him must be caught up by it. It was a force that struck deep into Jan's mind, bringing a tremor to her heart and a shiver to her skin. There was no denying it: if you came within Marc Tyrell's orbit, you had either to go along with him or positively oppose him—there could be no half measures. At the moment, because she was interested in the project and because her career depended on it, she wanted to go along with him. But suppose it became necessary to oppose him. . .?

Susan Cartwright would not have acknowledged any problem. But Jan knew that working with this man was not going to be easy. And if she couldn't face the consequences, now was the moment to make her decision. Stay—or back out.

Marc glanced up suddenly and caught her eyes on him. There was a moment of complete silence. Jan felt the tiny hairs at the back of her neck stiffen and rise. She stared into the grey eyes, held by something in their depths, something that she couldn't identify yet which struck a chord somewhere deep inside. Stay or back out, she thought in sudden panic. Stay. . .or back out.

And never know what it was to work with Marc Tyrell. Never know what it was that came from somewhere deep in those grey, unflinching eyes and spoke to something equally deep in herself.

She felt as much in danger as Sherlock Holmes had been in when he had stood on the edge of that Swiss precipice and plunged down over the tumbling falls into what his creator had hoped was oblivion. One false step and it could have been her fate too. . .and no clamouring public to bring her back to life.

One false step now. . .Stay—or back out.

'Well?' Marc said quietly, and again she had the unnerving sensation that he had read her mind. 'What's the verdict? Do you think you can work with me?'

It was the first time he had mentioned the subject since she had arrived—until then, he had appeared to be taking it for granted. *Had* he read her mind?

Jan swallowed. Her voice was husky. She tried to

speak, failed and then tried again, knowing that what she said now might affect the rest of her life.

'I think so. We—we seem to think along the same lines. As long as that continues——'

'You mean you'll chicken out of any arguments?'

'Not that at all,' Jan said sharply. 'If I don't agree with you I'll say so. And tell you why. If you don't like it——'

'I'll wait to be convinced,' he said equably. 'Look, Jan, let's get this straight. I'm not looking for a syco-phant. There are too many of them around as it is. I could walk out of this office now and come back with a dozen. That's why I asked Lucia to recommend some-one. At the same time—I don't want a hedgehog either.'

'What do you mean?'

'Someone who's all prickles. Someone who rolls up into an unapproachable little ball at the slightest touch. If you're going to be permitted to speak your mind, Jan, then so must I. Is that fair?'

'Yes, of course, but——'

'Right,' he said. 'Then I'll start now. There's one thing about you that I don't like and it could get in the way of the work, so I'll tell you at once. If you think it can be put right, well and good. We're in business. If not——' he snapped his fingers '—we forget the whole thing, right?'

Jan stared at him. To her dismay, she felt a hard knot of anxiety form somewhere in her chest. At that moment, she knew just how badly she wanted this job and how disappointed she would be if she didn't get it.

'What is it?' she asked.

'It's your general attitude towards men and your specific attitude towards me,' he said deliberately. 'And I realise that it may be something you can't help, considering who your mother is.' He looked exasperated at her obvious surprise. 'Surely you didn't imagine that I didn't know? Your mother's a household name, you must be aware of that. I've never met her, but I almost got the job of interviewing her once for a documentary—thank goodness, it fell through.' He stared at her speculatively for a moment, his fingers drumming lightly on the desk. 'Now look, Jan, I anticipated this problem when I considered you for this job, but your reputation as a researcher convinced me that I ought to give you a chance. And I think we could work well together, if only you can get your priorities sorted out.' He leaned forward. 'I've nothing against Women's Lib. But I don't like the over-strident female, the woman who puts up a barrier against every male she happens to encounter. The woman who sees a slight in every casual remark and every offhand gesture. Do you understand me?'

'No, I don't,' Jan said curtly. 'Women have had to fight to get where they are now. We're not going to start backing down at this stage. The very fact that you say what you've just said shows how defensive men are getting—scared of their own vulnerability, terrified that women are going to take over and treat them as they themselves have been treated for centuries. Well, if you want my opinion, I don't think it would do men one bit of harm to get a taste of the medicine they've been handing out. And it might be quite interesting to see just what the world is like with women running it!'

'Not a lot better, if history is anything to go by!' Marc snapped. 'Look back down the ages, Jan, and give me just one instance in which a powerful woman has been softer, more humane, than a man. Look at Cleopatra, Boadicea, Elizabeth the First, Lucrezia Borgia—they're lethal, more dangerous and ruthless than any man!

Equality? You're not looking for equality, any of you—
if you were, men would respect it. We'd like it! But we
know that once you get your foot in the door it's the end
for the human race. That's why we have to fight it—why
we fight you.'

Jan stared at him. Her lips tightened.

'Then that's all there is to be said, isn't it? You'd
better find someone else to do your researching.'

She stood up and turned away, unable to hide the
bitter disappointment she felt, knowing even now that
she'd longed to work on this project with the man who
was commonly agreed to be the most exciting director in
TV today. Yet what else could she have done? Going
against her own principles would have left her feeling
even worse. How could she have done that and continued
to live with herself?

She felt Marc's hand on her shoulder. It was warm
and firm. Gently he turned her to face him. 'Jan, Jan,'
he said quietly, and something within her stirred at the
deep softness of his voice. 'Look, let's start again, shall
we? I don't *want* to find anyone else. I want you on this
job. That's why I asked Lucia for you. I believe you'll
do it well, and I believe that once we get this sexist stuff
out of the way we can work well together. Why don't we
give it a try, hm?'

Jan stared up at him. His eyes were dark, intent, his
mouth serious. She removed her glance quickly from
those fine-chiselled lips—hadn't she read in some silly
magazine that if you wanted a man to kiss you, you
looked at his mouth. . .? She took a step backwards.

'What do you say?' he asked again, softly. 'We'll make
a bargain, OK? You want to be treated as one of the
boys, right?'

'That'll suit me very well,' Jan said stiffly.

'Then treat me the same,' he said. 'And any other man I have in my crew. We're not all out to rape every female we see, nor are we interested in putting them down as "little women". Just to do the job—which is all I'm asking you to do.'

Jan felt her anger rise again. 'If you think I'm likely to be a troublemaker, Mr Tyrell——'

'Oh, for goodness' sake,' he said irritably, 'sit down. Isn't this just what I'm talking about? Don't be so damned *defensive!*'

Slowly she sat down again and met his eyes. After a moment, her own dropped and she said, 'All right. But I can't promise never to disagree with you.'

'Did I ask you to? Look, Jan, we're going to fight a lot, you and I—I don't suffer fools gladly and when we're working I don't give any quarter. That's why we have to get things straight from the beginning, understand? And now. . .about this trip to Switzerland. How are you fixed for next week?'

Jan stared at him. 'Next *week*?'

'Why not? The sooner the better, and I find this idea of yours interesting. We won't be doing any filming, of course—it'll be just you and me, researching the area and bouncing ideas off each other. There's a lot of planning to do—we might as well use the travelling time to do some of it. Look, I'll get my secretary to fix things up and get in touch with you. Meanwhile, we can be sorting out some ideas for the shape of the programme— interviews, drama content and so on. OK?'

Jan nodded. Her mind was whirling. Switzerland— next week! She and Marc Tyrell, together in some of the most spectacular and romantic scenery she had ever known.

Not that romance would enter into it, of course. This

was a job of work, no more than that. And Jan wasn't interested in romance anyway. Her career was what mattered. And she and Marc had already agreed that their relationship was to be purely a business one.

All the same. . .the thought of the Jungfrau, flushed apricot with the soft alpenglow of sunset gleaming on its snowy peaks, rose like a talisman in her mind. And she carried it there as she left Marc's office and all through the following week, while she made her preparations for their journey.

Nobody was ever quite the same when they were in a foreign country. And the hidden undercurrents of energy, of danger, that she had sensed in Marc Tyrell might easily come to the fore.

Was she really going to be able to cope?

CHAPTER THREE

JAN and Marc arrived in Switzerland to a Swiss spring, with the last of the winter snows only two or three weeks behind, and the meadows heavy with the scent of newly opened flowers. Parking the car by the railway station in the valley town of Lauterbrunnen, they stared up at the towering mountains, their peaks gleaming with the snows that never melted, and held their ears against the roar of the waterfalls after which the village was named.

'What a place!' said Marc. 'You're right, Jan, this is going to make marvellous filming. Where do we catch the train for Mürren?'

'Over here.' She nodded at the station across the road, where the steep rack railway led up the cliff to Grütschalp and then along the edge of the precipice to Mürren itself. Since no cars were allowed there, everyone had to use the train; in the same way, visitors were also crowding on to the train which ran up the opposite side of the valley, to Wengen, and beyond that to the spectacular Jungfraujoch, the shoulder of the Jungfrau itself. Jan gave it a wistful glance, remembering the holiday she had spent here a few years ago and hoping there would be a chance to pay another visit.

So far, the trip had gone better than she had expected. They had flown to Zürich and picked up the hire car there, driving immediately to Lauterbrunnen. Jan had been forced to bite her tongue when she'd found Marc automatically taking the driver's seat, but had comforted herself with the knowledge that once they arrived in

Mürren the car would be left behind—and she, having been here before, would be the guide. And she'd had to admit that Marc was a good driver—fast but competent. As he would be, of course, being Marc Tyrell!

As yet there had been no sign of his famous irascible temper. But there'd been surprisingly little chance for casual conversation—on the plane, Marc had taken the opportunity to go over some of their joint ideas for the production, and during the drive from Zürich he'd made it clear that he didn't appreciate small talk while at the wheel. And Jan had been only too happy to confine her remarks to the directions she was giving from the map.

They boarded the train and she smiled to herself, conscious of the interested glances of the other passengers. At this time of day, most of them were local, going home to Mürren from jobs in the valley, or even further away at Interlaken. No doubt they were amused by Marc's luggage; he seemed to have brought everything but the kitchen sink, or whatever the bachelor equivalent of such a thing might be. The video gear, she knew, was to be used for recording items that he thought might make good film later, when the crew arrived. But as 'holiday snapshot' equipment, it certainly looked a bit over the top. She caught the eye of a man in the opposite seat and he smiled and nodded.

'You are on holiday, yes?'

'Well, not exactly—that is——'

His grin widened. 'Ach so! It is the special time, *ja*? The—I don't know the English word—*die Flitterwochen*. The holiday for when you are married.'

'The holiday for——' Jan stared at him, nonplussed, then realised suddenly what he meant and felt herself blush vividly. 'The *honeymoon*! No!' Involuntarily, she glanced at Marc and found him watching her with an amusement that brought an even deeper flush to her cheeks. 'Certainly not!' she exclaimed. '*Nein*! We're not married—*wir sind verheiratet nicht*—is that right?' She felt her cheeks burn as the whole carriage began to smile and turned again to Marc. 'And you're no help! Can't you tell them?'

'Tell them what?' he said, grinning. 'We're not on our honeymoon because we're not married. What else is there to say?'

'Tell them we're here to *work*,' she snapped, and turned back to the Swiss. '*Wir arbeiten*—I was never any good at these beastly German endings. *Mein Mann——*' too late she realised that this was also the German word for 'husband' '—*der Engländer ist das Fernsehen.*' At this, everyone exploded with laughter and the little carriage shook on its rails. 'Oh, *now* what have I said?' she exclaimed in exasperation.

'I think you've just told them I'm a television,' said Marc. 'And, judging by the interested looks I'm getting now, I should think they've interpreted that as a television *star* of some kind. So I suppose I can expect to be followed everywhere by autograph-hunters convinced that I'm someone straight out of *Dallas*, if they watch that here, and they probably do. Thanks a bunch, Jan.'

'Well, it's your own fault,' she said crossly, and turned to look out of the window. 'Oh, just look at that heavenly view!'

The carriages were built to fit the steepness of the hill, the seats facing up and down. Jan and Marc were seated on the upper side of their carriage, looking down over the heads of the people opposite. As the train rose steadily up the cliff, the view of the mountains increased dramatically; shining white peaks soaring above a dark blanket of conifers, the little town of Wengen clinging to the green hill on the other side of the valley.

'Imagine what it must have been like to live here years ago,' she said softly. 'Before tourists began to come. Just the farmers working their pastures, taking the cows up high in the mountains during the summer, coming down again when the snows began. So peaceful. . .'

'And damned hard work too,' Marc observed. 'Though there are still farmers who live like that. The countryside hasn't been entirely given over to toursim. And a good thing too—it would die if the old ways disappeared completely.'

From the tiny station at Grütschalp, the train ran along the edge of the plateau. It seemed to be heading directly for the jagged heights of the Jungfrau and its attendant mountains, the famous Monch, the Eiger and the Silberhorn—each one a Mecca for climbers. Jan sat close to the window, drinking in the view. She was aware of Marc beside her and wished fleetingly that their relationship could be different—something other than purely business. Inwardly, she smiled, picturing what her mother's reaction would be to such a sentiment. From babyhood, Jan had been brought up to be scornful of 'romance' and all that implied. 'Let a man into your life and it's no longer your own,' Susan Cartwright had said over and over again, ignoring the fact that her own husband could scarcely be said to have taken over her life. 'Women are still expected to submit. All through the ages, men have dominated society, and it's up to us to redress the balance.'

Up till now, Jan had to admit, Marc Tyrell hadn't tried to dominate her—perhaps because so far their ideas had been in accord. But she had no illusions; once they did begin to disagree—as they must, some time—she

knew that he would show his true colours. And then she
would need all her resources to stand up against him.

'Right, let's get this stuff unloaded.' The train had
arrived at Mürren and people were gathering their bags
together. Marc picked up his suitcase and camera equipment. 'Can you manage the rest, Jan? How far's our
hotel, do you know? Can we get one of those trolleys to
transport the gear?'

'I should think so.' She hefted the rest of the luggage,
thinking wryly that this was somewhere that Women's
Lib fell down. Once upon a time, a woman wouldn't
have been allowed to lift more than a finger to summon
help. . . She struggled to get the remaining suitcases and
assorted bags off the train and looked up in surprise as a
brown hand reached out for the heaviest case and
removed it firmly from her grasp. A pair of deep blue
eyes twinkled into hers and white teeth flashed in a
suntanned face.

'Allow me, *Fräulein*,' said a deep, pleasantly musical
voice. 'You look far too delicate for such a heavy
burden.'

Startled, Jan stepped back, inadvertently relinquish-
ing the suitcase. She stared at the man who was now
swinging it easily to the platform and then turning for
the rest of her baggage. He was tall—as tall as Marc, she
guessed—and as blond as Marc was dark. A tinge of
Swiss accent gave his voice a quality that was immediately distinctive. He was wearing the dark suit of a
businessman, but the easy, muscular grace with which
he handled the suitcases hinted at a body that was
accustomed to much hard exercise—climbing, skiing,
perhaps even more daring sports such as hang-gliding or
parasailing.

'There.' He was on the platform now, smiling up at

her. 'And now for you, *Fraülein*.' And before Jan could
protest, she felt two strong hands at her waist and found
herself lifted down from the train as easily as if she were
a child.

Flushed and confused, she looked up into the blue
eyes and then, hastily, away again—and straight into
Marc's.

'Well,' he remarked with an odd edge to his voice,
'maybe I was wrong after all—maybe you *do* like to have
doors opened for you.'

Jan felt her colour deepen. She looked up at the Swiss
again and began to stammer her thanks. But he cut her
short with an easy gesture and turned slightly to include
Marc in his words.

'Forgive me, I had no idea you were escorted. I would
not have intruded. . . But you will allow me to remark
that you have a great deal more luggage than most
holiday-makers.'

'That's because we're not most holiday-makers,' Marc
said tersely. 'In fact, we're not on holiday at all. We're
here to work. So if you'll excuse us——'

'But of course,' the stranger said smoothly. 'As I said,
I have no wish to intrude. But if there's any help I can
offer you. . . You are strangers in Mürren, I take it?'

'I've been here before, a few years ago,' Jan volun-
teered, finding her voice again. The stranger's actions
had taken her so completely by surprise that she had
been unable to react at all—but now indignation was
warming her blood and she was as eager as Marc to get
rid of this too good-looking, too self-assured Swiss. 'But
I didn't stay here—I stayed in Wengen. And if you
could just tell us where the Hotel Sonnschein is. . .'

'The Sonnschein? You stay there? Then there is
nothing easier. Please wait one moment.' With a little

bow, he turned sharply and walked away. Marc moved closer to Jan and looked down at her.

'Well, you've certainly made a hit there,' he muttered. 'And it looks like he's gone down well with you too— you let him manhandle you then as if you'd known him for years! Just don't forget we're here to work, all right?'

'Did I ever suggest anything else?' Jan retorted, her colour still high. 'As for letting him manhandle me—I didn't have much chance to prevent him. And *you* weren't going to offer any help, were you?'

'Only because you gave me to understand you'd prefer to be treated as one of the boys. But there are clearly boys and boys.' Marc's voice was edged with sharpness, and Jan gave him a curious look. Why was he so rattled about this? 'Anyway, let's forget it and get this gear shifted before your Swiss charmer comes back—oh, damn!'

Jan stifled a giggle. The platform had been empty, but even as Marc bent to lift the cases again the tall Swiss reappeared, striding purposefully towards them. Following him was a muscular youth in shorts, already carrying the small suitcase which was all the Swiss appeared to have with him. At a nod from the older man, the youth bent and lifted Jan's cases easily, hitching one under his arm and bending again to lift Marc's video equipment.

'Here, you can leave that alone!' Marc stepped forward quickly. 'That's valuable—I'll carry it, if you don't mind.' He glanced at the Swiss. 'Look, it's good of you to offer to help, but we can manage perfectly well. If you'd just tell us which way to go to our hotel——'

'But there's no need.' The smile flashed charmingly. 'I am going there myself, and Hans will be happy to help carry your bags. It is no more than a few steps—you will see.' He lifted Jan's second case and turned to follow the youth, who was already setting off towards the exit. 'Follow me, please.'

Jan glanced at Marc. 'We might as well do as we're told,' she said with resignation. 'He's got my luggage now—I'm not letting that out of my sight. Come on, Marc.'

Marc grunted and picked up his video case. 'Well, if he *wants* to carry complete strangers' luggage. . . But after this, we're going to shake him off, Jan, I'm warning you. It's easy to see what he's after and I don't want to lose my researcher before we even start work.'

'And do you imagine I'm just going to fold up and let him have his wicked way with me?' Jan stalked angrily beside him, as they left the station to find themselves in the quiet road that led into the village itself. 'Do you really think I've got this far without ever having to fend off unwelcome male attentions? I've had quite a lot of experience—and I don't intend to give way now.'

'They didn't look all that unwelcome to me,' muttered Marc. 'You were ready to swoon into his arms if he'd wanted you to.'

'I was *not*! I was just taken by surprise.'

'Well, make sure you don't get taken by anything else,' he growled as they drew level with the Swiss, who was now waiting outside the main door of the hotel that stood beside the road. Jan turned deliberately away from Marc, gave him a charming smile and said in her normal clear voice, 'So this is the Sonnschein! It looks lovely, and what a beautiful position. I wonder if my room will look at that marvellous view across the valley.'

'If it doesn't,' the Swiss said, 'we shall change it at once.' He bowed. 'Allow me to introduce myself—Kurt Brunner, at your service. If there's anything you need during your stay here, I hope you will let me know personally. And now, let's go inside and find out just which rooms you have been assigned.'

Jan gave Marc a bemused look and followed him. Hans was already inside with their luggage piled beside the reception desk. The girl behind it looked up and smiled, speaking to Kurt Brunner in German. Almost immediately Jan found herself lost, but at the end of the conversation Kurt Brunner turned and gave her a small bow.

'So! That is all perfectly satisfactory, Miss Cartwright. Your room has been changed from one facing the road to one overlooking the valley, with a balcony.' His blue eyes flicked over Marc. 'I take it that you are happy enough with the arrangements already made for you, Mr Tyrell,' he said smoothly. 'Or do you wish an alteration also?'

'Not at all,' Marc said stiffly. 'As I've just reminded Jan, we're here to work. Anyway, what gives you so much influence here—and how do you know our names?'

Amusement touched the tanned face. 'I must admit to a certain amount of influence, it is true, but that is only because I am the owner. As to your names—that is simple. I knew you were expected and you were the only new arrivals on the train. But anyway, your names are displayed on your luggage—*nicht wahr?*' His smile revealed perfect white teeth. 'And now Hans will take your cases to your room, Mr Tyrell, except for the valuable equipment which I know you like to carry yourself. And, Miss Cartwright—if you will allow me. . .?'

He bent and lifted Jan's cases, turning away towards the lift before Marc could register a protest. Jan gave the blond Swiss a slightly stunned look. He certainly knew how to take charge! She felt a rising admiration for him—any man who could score over Marc Tyrell just had to be admired. Even if he did have the kind of over-glossy good looks that you might expect to find on a film set rather than in a hotel in a tiny Swiss mountain resort. . .

'Well, go on, then,' Marc said testily. 'Follow your leader. At least we can get ourselves sorted out, now we're here.'

Jan grinned and stepped into the lift where Kurt Brunner was already waiting for her. It was as tiny as most hotel lifts—there was barely room for the two of them with all her luggage, and she found herself standing rather closer to him than she would normally have chosen. Keeping her eyes down, she was aware of the musky odour of his aftershave and the warmth of his body. She was also aware of his cool blue eyes, resting on her with frank appraisal. After a moment, she lifted her own glance to meet his. They held the look for several seconds, then the lift stopped.

Kurt Brunner slid back the door and Jan stepped out, feeling slightly breathless.

'All our best rooms are on this floor,' he observed, leading her along a carpeted passage and producing a key. 'And this is the best of them all—your own small suite.' He unlocked the door and stepped back with a flourish. 'I hope you will like it.'

Jan walked into the room and stopped with a gasp. 'It's wonderful!' She stared at the huge patio window which revealed the range of mountains across the valley; a staggering panorama of soaring white peaks, gleaming white in the afternoon sunshine, and jagged crags adding a menacing touch of deep, shadowy black to the shim-mering beauty. Above them, the sky was a pale, ethereal blue which deepened to intense navy at the zenith, broken only by one faint drift of white cloud, as insubstantial as a wisp of chiffon torn from a bridal veil.

'I can't believe it,' said Jan, going over to the window, which was drawn back so that she could walk straight out on to the balcony. 'I shall never be able to stop looking. I've never seen anything so lovely.'

'It is a fine view,' Kurt acknowledged with a smile. 'We are as proud of it as if we had fashioned it ourselves. . . And the room, does that meet with your approval?'

'The room?' Jan turned quickly. Stunned by the view which lay outside, she had scarcely noticed the room itself. Now she saw the big double bed, the thick white carpet, the furnishings, which were so much more than adequate yet so discreet; as well as the bed and wardrobe, there was a full-sized dressing-table and, at the window end of the room, a sitting area with two armchairs and a large coffee-table. The whole room was furnished in a delicate, watery green, with walls a white as sparkling as that of the mountains outside.

Still moving in a daze, she crossed to look at the bathroom, noting that its pale green and white décor matched exactly that of the bedroom. As well as the bath, there was a shower compartment; the floor was tiled in patterned ceramic tiles and a pile of fluffy towels were neatly folded on the unit beside the large washbasin.

'Approval?' she repeated, returning to the bedroom and crossing once again to the window. 'It's simply wonderful! But there must be some mistake, Herr Brunner. I wasn't supposed to have a room like this. We booked two single rooms, at economy price. I shall have to change.'

'And why, pray?' He took her arm gently in a firm, warm clasp and led her out to the balcony. 'Listen, Miss Cartwright, the room is vacant. It was booked for a month by an old and valued customer and now she cannot use it—a sudden illness in the family. It is unlikely that it would be booked again, for it is used almost exclusively by our regular clients, those who wish something a little more luxurious than our normal rooms. So why should I not let it to someone who I can see will appreciate it? It is my prerogative to do that I think, *nicht wahr?*'

They were standing side by side at the rail of the balcony. Jan looked down, deep into the gorge that slashed through the mountains. She looked again at the vastness of the range opposite, the Jungfrau, the Monch, the Eiger, and her senses swam.

'I like my hotel to be enjoyed by those who stay here,' Kurt's deep voice said softly in her ear. 'And I like to give something extra to those who have the sensitivity to appreciate it. You will allow me this small pleasure, I hope?'

Jan looked again at the soaring mountains and took hold of herself. Allow him this small pleasure indeed! And what 'small pleasure' would he be demanding next? She cast a quick glance back through the glass door to the big double bed. . . No, much as she hated to admit it, Marc was right about this man. He was making his intentions blatantly obvious, and it was up to her to make her own responses just as clear. She couldn't possibly accept this room, and she must tell him so at once.

She looked up into Kurt Brunner's smiling, confident face, and opened her mouth to speak.

'Well, *you* certainly seem to have fallen on your feet!'

Marc's voice cut savagely across the moment, and she leapt away from Kurt like a scalded cat. 'The best room in the hotel, or I'm a yeti's grandmother. What do you think this is going to cost us, for heaven's sake?' He stormed through the room and came to rest on the balcony, glaring at Jan with angry, iron-grey eyes. 'You ought to have more sense!' He turned to Kurt Brunner. 'Look, I'm sorry, but there's been some mistake. Miss Cartwright can't possibly have this room. The budget won't run to it. TV companies aren't made of money, you know, at least this one isn't. We have to be careful with our pennies, we're not shooting *Dallas*!'

Kurt smiled. 'Please don't worry, Mr Tyrell. I've already explained to Miss Cartwright that there will be no extra charge. The room is vacant anyway. You are satisfied with your own, I take it?'

'Perfectly,' Marc said stiffly. 'It's what I wanted—adequate. That's all we need. *Both* of us.' He turned to Jan. 'Your room should have been the one next to mine. We'll move your things down straight away.'

Immediately Jan's anger flared. Who did he think he was, ordering her about? 'Oh, will we?' she countered, lifting her chin. 'And what if I don't want to? What if I'd rather stay here?' She met his hard, angry glance with one of her own, steely and defiant. 'So long as it doesn't affect the budget, I don't see what business it is of yours where I sleep.' The double meaning in her words brought fresh colour storming into her cheeks, but she turned to Kurt and went on quickly, 'I'll be very happy to use this room, Herr Brunner. It's kind of you to offer it.'

'Please. Let's say no more about it.' Kurt lifted a graceful brown hand. 'The bill will be as you expected it to be. But let's not think of your leaving yet.' His smile was warm, almost caressing. 'I am sure you have much to discuss with your colleague. But I will be honoured if you would—both—have a drink with me in the lounge before dinner. Shall we say at seven?' He inclined his head towards Marc and left them, walking with easy strides back through the bedroom. Jan stared after him. Her pulse, she discovered, was racing.

Almost stiffly, she turned her head back to look at Marc and found him watching her with a cynical expression that immediately got under her skin.

'Well, there's no need to look like that!' she snapped. 'And you can just stop thinking——'

'Thinking what?'

'Whatever it is you *are* thinking! It doesn't take much imagination to know what that is. Look, he's told me, the room's unexpectedly vacant and unlikely to be let again at once. He just thought I'd enjoy it, that's all. And I shall,' she finished defiantly.

'I bet you will.' Marc turned and gave the room, with its king-sized bed, a comprehensive glance. 'You looked as if you'd already begun, when I arrived.'

'And just what's that supposed to mean?'

'Oh, for goodness' sake, Jan! Don't play the little innocent with me. The man fancies you and you fancy him right back. Look at the way you let him lift you down from the train! You'd have chewed me up into little pieces if I'd tried that. And carrying your bags— after all your high-flown talk about equality and being one of the boys! Look, he's got one reason for giving you this room and one reason only—he wants to get you into that sumptuous white bed in there. And by the look in your eye, I'd say he's going to have no trouble at all. And he's made quite sure that I'm safely out of the way by giving me a box that would be privileged to be used as a broom-cupboard, two floors down and on the other side of the building.'

'And why should he imagine that you're likely to be *in* the way?' Jan asked freezingly. 'Just supposing that your disgusting assumptions were correct—which I can assure you they are *not*.'

'Knowledge of the human race, I guess,' Marc said bluntly. 'Put a man and a woman together in a hotel in a romantic setting like this, and the outcome's almost a foregone conclusion. And Kurt Brunner's like the rest of us—takes his opportunities where and when they occur.'

Jan stared at him. A feeling of loathing crept over her body like a second and repulsive skin. 'What a revolting man you are,' she said slowly. 'And what a revolting view you have of human nature. Well, let me tell you something. Whatever your own personal morals are—if morals is the right word for them—we don't all share them. All right, so I'm human and I have all the normal human drives and emotions. But I don't go round looking for opportunities to satisfy them with every attractive male I happen to meet. I have rather more self-respect than that. And now, if you don't mind, we'll leave all personal matters alone. We're here to work, as you so gallantly reminded me, and beyond discussing that I'd rather have nothing to do with you. Since this room is going to cost 90s-TV no more than your broom-cupboard, I'll be more than happy to keep it. And I'll be grateful if you'd leave it now—I want to unpack. As a matter of fact, I don't actually recall having invited you in.'

Marc's eyes sparked like flints striking fire. His face hardened, his lips forming a thin, angry line. He took a step forward and Jan felt his hands on her shoulders.

She could feel the fury vibrating through his fingers and she cast a nervous glance down into the chasm that lay beneath them. But when he spoke, his voice was oddly quiet, coming between gritted teeth.

'You little vixen!' he growled. 'I'll remind you who happens to be in charge of this expedition! You're working for *me*, remember? And you'll go along with what I say. All right, so you keep the room. But since it's so sumptuous we'll use it for any discussions we need to have about the job, and I'll consider it my right to come in and out as I please. Except when you're in bed, of course,' he added silkily. 'I wouldn't dream of intruding then.'

'If you're still implying——' Jan began hotly, but he cut in and drowned her words.

'Read what you like into what I say, my dear. As they say, if the cap fits. . . But just in case our Swiss hotelier *does* have any ideas and you should be tempted to accommodate him—why not have a taste of what else you might be missing?'

Before Jan could move, he had slipped his hands from her shoulders and drawn her into his arms. So suddenly that she gasped, she found her body crushed against his. Angrily, she opened her mouth to protest—and found her lips taken instead by the hard, possessive mouth of Marc Tyrell.

The kiss was a savage one. It took her like a storm, blasting away all her strength, killing any possibility of resistance. She felt her blood roar in her ears, felt her body weaken, Marc's power driving out any ability she had to deny him. As his tongue probed her mouth, she knew a moment of terror; and then, so quickly that she wondered if she had imagined that brief flash of fear, it was followed by a tenderness that made her tremble, a deep searching passion that brought the warmth surging back into her shaking limbs.

Marc let her go. He looked into her eyes.

'I'll see you downstairs,' he said, and abruptly turned and left her.

CHAPTER FOUR

JAN opened her eyes slowly, reluctantly, even the dazzling sight of the mountains outside failing to lift her spirits after an almost sleepless night. She lay for a few moments staring mistily at them, but it wasn't the soaring beauty of the glittering peaks that she saw; it was the darkness of Marc Tyrell's face and the sardonic glint of his flint-grey eyes. And on her lips, still burning through to her soul, was the feel of his kiss.

She turned her head quickly, muffling her groan on her pillow, wishing for the thousandth time that she could simply blot the memory from her mind. But it was as clear and vivid now as it had been at midnight last night—at one, two, three in the morning. The initial savagery—the slow, amazing transformation to a tenderness that had seemed to surprise him as much as it had her; the anger she had felt in both him and herself, and the totally unexpected sweetness.

This was crazy! With a violent jerk, Jan sat up in bed and ran trembling fingers through her tangled curls. All right, so Marc Tyrell had kissed her—was that any such big deal? She didn't want him to, she didn't even like him—but she had been kissed unwillingly before, once or twice, by men she didn't like, and it had never had this effect on her. Normally in such situations she'd been well able to take care of herself, making it absolutely clear to the man concerned that his attentions weren't welcome and then putting the whole distasteful episode out of her mind. But this time. . .

This time it was different. She'd been with Marc Tyrell long enough to know that she respected him, even if she didn't like him. And his kiss hadn't been that of an opportunist, snatching at a chance in a dark corner or at a Christmas party. It had been designed to tell her something—to make a point. To show her, in fact, that Marc Tyrell would be a better lover than Kurt. And lastly—a point she admitted only with great reluctance and out of a sense that where Marc Tyrell was concerned she had to be entirely honest with herself—it *hadn't* been distasteful.

She sat quite still among the foam of sheets, considering. Just why should Marc want to display to her his prowess as a lover? Was it just the parading of male attractions, like stags strutting before a gathering of hinds? Or was there something more?

And did he realise the effect his kiss had had on her?

Jan shivered suddenly. If only she'd had time to prepare herself! If only she could have guarded against that sudden storm invading her body, the reeling shock that had knocked cold any chance of resisting him before his lips had gentled against hers, warming her trembling heart, bringing a hint of sensations that were wholly new, wholly delightful.

But if she had been able to protect herself. . .she would never have experienced it.

And wouldn't that have been better? she asked the towering mountains. Wasn't it better never to know what lay beyond such insurmountable barriers?

But the mountains stared back, impassive and serene, and gave no answer.

Jan was in the breakfast-room first, pointedly studying her notes, when Marc arrived. Sitting gazing at the silent mountains was no use, she had decided at last, and had thrust aside the bedclothes, showered and dressed, determined that she was not going to let Marc throw her. The kiss had happened and it was over. End of story. Any effect it might have had on her was to remain her secret.

She glanced up, keeping her expression casual, as Marc helped himself to croissants and coffee from the buffet and came to sit opposite her.

'Oh, hello. I was just having a look through these notes. You know, I keep thinking there's a detective we've missed—a modern writer, not one of the classics, yet I get the feeling he's not a modern detective. Is there anyone we've not thought of—Rendell, Francis, Marsh—surely we've covered them all?'

Her voice was a little too hurried and she caught Marc's eye and glanced hastily away, uncomfortably aware that he knew just what she was doing. But when he spoke his own tone was even.

'Never mind that for the moment, Jan. There's something I want to say to you. Last night——'

'Yes?' She spoke more sharply than she'd intended to, and felt the colour come to her cheeks. 'Did you sleep well, Marc? In your—your broom-cupboard? I hope your bed was comfortable.'

'Very, thank you. But that's not what I wanted to talk about.' He leaned across the table, his eyes dark as shadowed snow. 'Look, I think we should talk about——'

'*I* think we should talk about the programme,' Jan said positively. 'After all, it's what we're here for, isn't it? And I'm really not awfully interested in anything else.'

'Not even Swiss hoteliers?' His voice was suddenly sharp, and she felt the familiar anger rise in her and welcomed it. As long as they were quarrelling, she felt safe—there was no chance of that strange tenderness which had frightened her so much.

'I meant, of course, in anything else that *you* might want to talk about,' she said smoothly, and saw him flinch slightly. 'Our relationship is strictly business, after all, and I'm perfectly happy to keep it that way—aren't you?'

He stared at her for a moment and she held his gaze, ignoring the sense that his eyes were giving her messages she didn't want to read. After a moment there was a tiny, almost imperceptible change in his expression and he shrugged.

'All right, Jan, have it your own way. Strictly business. So long as we can stay on friendly terms—it's impossible to work together if we don't.

'But of course,' she agreed smilingly. 'Why ever not?'

Marc grunted and began to spread jam on his croissant. And Jan sipped her coffee, feeling that for once she had won. This round was scored to her.

So why didn't she feel more pleased about it? Why did she feel that instead of winning something, she had lost it? And why were they scoring off each other anyway?

The cable car going to the top of the Schilthorn rose straight up the mountainside from Mürren to the summit. It almost brushed the tops of growing trees and bushes, swayed high above deep-cut valleys, swung perilously close to sheer, jagged rockfaces. Near the top, it swung across snowfields, and when Jan and Marc emerged beside the Piz Gloria revolving restaurant they shivered in the sudden freshness of the clear air.

'How high are we?' asked Marc. 'Ten thousand feet? Well, no wonder we feel the difference—it's nearly twice

as high as Mürren. All the same, you should watch out
for sunburn, Jan—it's really quite hot and the air's so
unpolluted you could burn in seconds.'

She gave him a withering glance and led the way from
the cable car platform to the large terrace. Did he really
think she needed taking care of, like a child out with its
father. . .? And then she stopped short, all irritation
driven from her mind at the prospect before her.

The round, revolving restaurant of Piz Gloria, the
highest in the world, was poised on the very tip of the
soaring peak of the Schilthorn. And all around, in every
direction, lay the Swiss Alps—mile upon mile of snow-
covered mountains, their summits slicing into the deep
blue of the sky with a succession of jagged spires and
beacons of crystalline ice.

'Well!' Marc said in her ear. 'Have you ever seen
anything quite so spectacular? You're right, Jan—we've
got to film here.' He stood beside her, turning slowly to
take in the entire panoramic view. 'No wonder they had
to make the restaurant revolve! Let's go inside and have
lunch—it's got to be an experience, seeing all this wheel
slowly by.'

'It takes about an hour to go right round,' said Jan,
following him into the light, airy restaurant. 'Look,
there are seats at that table, right next to the window—
let's sit there. Only don't put your camera on the
window-sill—it's only the inside that actually revolves.'

'And just the strip nearest the window, at that.' Marc
took his seat and Jan sat down facing him. 'Don't the
waitresses ever lose their customers? By the time they
come out with an order, you're nowhere near where you
were to start with!'

Jan laughed. 'They seem to know how to find the
right tables.' She gazed out of the window, drinking in

the expansive views. 'I wonder if they ever get used to it all.'

'If they do, they must find valley living tame in comparison. Imagine going to work by bus again once you've been used to using the cable car. And looking up instead of down. No, I should think living up here could become quite addictive. A really rarefied atmosphere.' Marc glanced across the table at Jan and added quietly, 'It's surprising, the things that can become necessary to one's well-being. Jan——'

'Hello!' she interrupted him, her eye catching that of a new arrival in the restaurant. 'Look who's here! Kurt—how nice to see you!'

She was conscious of Marc's instant withdrawal, but dismissed it. His male ego again, she supposed—the desire to be in charge, thwarted by Kurt's generosity. Well, that was just stupid! And typical of a man, as her mother would have been the first to point out. They always needed to be in competition with each other, didn't they—always had to be top dog?

It had been equally obvious yesterday evening, as they sat together in the lounge before dinner. Smooth as Kurt had been, his every remark had been met by Marc with a rejoinder so terse as to be almost blatantly rude. So that Jan had felt compelled to make up for it by behaving with a bright chattiness that wasn't really her at all—and, resenting that and resenting even more the irony in Marc's eyes as he watched her, had been goaded into a flirtatiousness that made her blush now to recall it.

It would have served her right if Kurt *had* turned up at her bedroom door later, as Marc so evidently believed he would. And she still wasn't sure why he hadn't, though she was thankful enough at the reprieve. Fending off Kurt's advances when she was uncomfortably aware

that she'd probably encouraged them wouldn't have been
fun.

All in all, she thought, gazing out of the window at
the spectacular panorama wheeling slowly past, she'd be
quite glad to leave Mürren and go on to Meiringen,
where they were to see the Reichenbach Falls. And that,
when she'd looked forward so much to being here, was
yet another thorn in her side—pushed there, of course,
by Marc Tyrell.

Kurt was coming over to them, his eyes on her, his
face alight with pleasure.

'Ah, Jan—and Mr Tyrell,' he said, coming over to
them. 'What a fortunate meeting! I was sorry not to see
you this morning, but some rather urgent business
cropped up—however, perhaps we may lunch together
now, in these beautiful surroundings.'

'Sorry, no,' Marc said before Jan could reply. 'This is
very much a working lunch, Herr Brunner—I'm sure
you understand, being a businessman yourself. Work
must come before pleasure sometimes, mustn't it?' He
gave the other man a grin that reminded Jan forcibly of
a wolf about to attack a rival predator. 'Nice to see you,
of course. I take it you own this place as well?'

'Alas, no!' Kurt looked rueful. 'Much as I would like
to. . . But the owner is in fact a close friend of mine and
we were to lunch together. I have only just discovered
that he too has been called away on business. But no
matter. I shall sit over there, just a few tables away so as
not to disturb you from your talk, and when you have
finished perhaps you would join me for coffee, yes?'

'I doubt if we'll have time,' said Marc. 'Jan and I have
rather a lot to get through—we have to decide all kinds
of things, what exactly we're to film, what shots to try,

all that kind of thing. I imagine it will take us the rest of the day.'

Kurt bowed. 'Then tonight, perhaps, for a drink before dinner. I wanted to tell you how much I enjoyed last night.' His eyes rested on Jan as he spoke and she felt her cheeks colour slightly. 'It would be a great pleasure to me to repeat it,' he said softly and, with another small bow, left them and went to sit some distance away.

'And just what did he mean by that?' Marc demanded at once.

'By what?'

'Oh, don't play the wide-eyed innocent! By "I wanted to tell you how much I enjoyed last night", of course. And how great a pleasure it would be to repeat it. Repeat what? Just what went on between you two?'

Jan stared at him, her heart hammering with fury. *Nothing* went on between us! He simply meant the talk we all had before dinner. And that's all. There isn't anything else to repeat. Look, he simply enjoyed talking to people who are really interested in the area, there's nothing more to it than that. It's only your disgusting mind that reads any more into what he's said or done.'

'Only my realistic mind,' he corrected her. 'Look, Jan, I told you yesterday, I'm not still wet behind the ears. I *know* what goes on in the world. And especially in *our* world, the one you and I inhabit. TV people get around. We live in an unreal atmosphere. We spend most of our time on a high—we're inclined to react faster than most people. We're more quickly attracted to each other, we respond and do something about it when it happens. There isn't time to let things develop slowly.' He leaned forward. 'You'll see a lot of this Brunner guy in the next couple of weeks, and then nothing. Do you really expect me to believe you'll pass up the chance of a quick whirl? And as for him——'

'No, never mind him!' Jan was white with anger, her topaz eyes blazing. 'Let's stick with what you're saying about me. It seems you think I've got the morals of an alley-cat. As if I'll go to bed with any passably good-looking stranger who gives me the come-on. Just what makes you think that, Marc Tyrell? What evidence do you have for believing that of me? I'd like to hear it.'

'Do I need evidence? You work in TV, don't you? You believe in some so-called equality, and I don't doubt for one minute that you believe in sexual freedom too. Can you deny any of that? Can you?'

'I——' She stopped and bit her lip. 'No, I can't deny any of that. I don't *want* to deny it. Yes, I work in TV— so do you. But that's nothing to do with it. You're implying that anyone who works in TV will sleep around, and that's nothing but a slander. Yes, I believe in equality. And yes, if that means women are entitled to the same sexual freedom that men have enjoyed for centuries, I believe in that too. If they want to take advantage of it. It doesn't mean that I want to do it myself. I don't believe that all men do, either. So now where's your evidence?'

Marc laughed, a short, bitter sound. 'Look, Jan, let's stop kidding, shall we? All right, what you say is plausible enough, I'll agree. So not all women in TV eat men for breakfast—so not all monkeys eat bananas. And your relationship with Kurt Brunner is as pure as the snow on those mountains wheeling past us at this very moment, and I've certainly no evidence that you'll go to bed with *every* man you meet. In fact, I can prove to my own satisfaction that you don't. I just wish you'd be a bit more discriminating.'

The restaurant was revolving very slowly. Whenever Jan glanced out of the window, it was at a different panorama of mountains. A few tables away she could see the back of Kurt's blond head. There was something on the window-sill not very far away; she saw a man pick it up, glance at it and then, smiling, replace it. She looked at Marc and knew a frustration so intense that she wanted to strangle him. Why *wouldn't* he believe her? And why did it seem so important that he did? Why couldn't she just not care?

'What do you mean by discriminating?' she asked in a low, tense voice.

'Why, you talk so much about equality.' He was smiling now, at ease, and she hated him for it. 'Yet here you are, falling for the oldest tricks in the book. All that carrying of cases, lifting you down from the train—I'd have expected you to feel humiliated by that, and angry. Yet you lapped it up.' He leaned forward. 'Can't you see, all the time you're accusing me of chauvinism, it's Kurt who's the real sexist. He's using all the old wiles to make you fall for him—appealing directly to the feminine side of you that you most want to deny. You want to be treated as one of the boys, you've said so, and you prickle like a porcupine if I offer so much as a hand, because we work together and you're on edge all the time to see that I don't take advantage of you. But he comes along with his shiny capped teeth and his sunbed bronze and gives you the old-fashioned treatment, and you fall for it like a ton of bricks.' He sat back, shaking his head gently. 'I'm disappointed in you, I really am.'

The object was nearer her now and someone else had picked it up. Whatever it was seemed amusing; the woman now holding it glanced around and caught her eye, smiling. Briefly, Jan wondered what it was, but it couldn't hold her attention; she was too enraged by what Marc was saying—and too disturbed.

But it just wasn't true! She *didn't* find Kurt attractive—she didn't 'lap up' his attentions. To be honest, she was slightly repelled by his suave charm—she much preferred a slightly abrasive irony, an acceptance of her as a person who needed no special treatment yet deserved respect, the apparently casual yet essentially caring attitude of a man who wouldn't fuss her but would provide a rock-like strength to lean on if ever she should need it. . . Abruptly, she flicked the thoughts away. They were too dangerous, begging questions she didn't want to answer.

She looked at Marc and knew that she couldn't really blame him for thinking the things he did. Hadn't she done her damnedest to give him just the impression she was now so indignant about? But that didn't mean he had to *believe* it, she thought illogically, and knew that her anger was mostly with herself for allowing herself to be driven into this corner. And if it hadn't been for Marc Tyrell, twisting everything, she'd never have got into this idiotic position—oh, he was *infuriating*!

'Kurt doesn't have capped teeth,' she said, knowing even as she said it how inadequate an answer it was. 'And he doesn't get his tan from a sunbed,' she added defiantly, and felt her face turn scarlet as Marc flung back his head in a shout of laughter.

'Oh, Jan, Jan, you slay me!' His face alight with open amusement, he reached across the table and took her hand. 'Look, let's stop this sparring, shall we? We really do have work to do and we get on best when we're doing it. Forget Kurt Brunner for a while—I'll be only too pleased to—and let's concentrate on the matter in hand.'

Jan looked down at the hand that clasped hers, firm

and warm. She remembered the kiss he had given her
yesterday, the savage attack that had melted into tenderness, and she felt a sudden sting in her eyes. Yes, it
would be nice to forget Kurt—to start again. And she
sensed a melting in her heart; a strange warmth that
began, disconcertingly, to spread through her whole
body.

As the inner platform of the restaurant had circled
slowly around, the object on the window-sill had now
come within reach of their table. Hazily, looking for
something—anything—to divert her attention, Jan
reached out and picked it up.

It was a white rose, taken from one of the vases that
stood on each table. Attached to it was a scrap of white
paper. It bore nothing but two names.

'Jan—Kurt.'

She read it slowly, then looked up and met Marc's
eyes. And recoiled from the contempt she saw there.

The hotel lounge was a long panelled room with windows
looking directly on to the view that Jan had from her
bedroom. Small groups of armchairs were placed so as
to take the best advantage of this view. In one corner
was the inevitable tiled stove, although she guessed that
the hotel was kept warm in winter by an efficient central
heating system that would make the stove little more
than ornamental.

When she came down for dinner that evening, Kurt
Brunner was already there, chatting with some other
guests. He excused himself and came over to lead her to
an armchair.

'This is the most comfortable, I think. And what will
you have to drink? One of my own cocktails, perhaps? I
think you'll enjoy that.'

'That sounds wonderful.' Jan sank into the armchair and gazed out at the mountains, still entranced by their serene majesty. Nothing could ever disturb their peace, she thought dreamily. All man's puny wars and quarrels would pass unnoticed by this gleaming, untouchable immensity. . . She looked up and smiled as Kurt returned and handed her a tall, cool glass.

'Let us drink to a happy stay for you,' he said, sitting down opposite her. 'The first of many, perhaps. Tell me how you enjoyed the Schilthorn. You have been there before, I believe.'

'Yes, two or three years ago—I spent a holiday in Wengen with an old schoolfriend and we came over one day and went up the Schilthorn in the cable car. It was cloudy that time, so we couldn't see much. But just now and then the clouds lifted, like——'

'Like pulling a curtain.' He nodded. 'I too have been on the summit of Schilthorn in such weather. In some ways, it is the most dramatic of all. First there is nothing but grey, swirling cloud and then—quite suddenly— there is a rent in the greyness, a shaft of blue sky and sunlight, and one catches a glimpse, the merest glimpse it may be, of the grandeur that lies all around. It is like a revelation of paradise, a hint to give mortals hope.' His blue eyes smiled. 'For some, of course, it may be frightening. Not everyone loves the magnificence of our scenery, you understand. Some find it daunting, they are overwhelmed by it. It is as if they feel the mountains diminish them, and they resent and fear them.'

'I don't see you fearing anything,' Jan remarked, and Kurt inclined his head a little.

'Physical dangers—the landscape, the elements—no. But I too am human, Jan. I too have my vulnerabilities. Such dangers as love and rejection—these I fear.'

Again his eyes met hers, in a long look. Jan felt herself held by them, then glanced away. Marc was right about Kurt, damn him—the Swiss was making it as plain as he knew how that he found her attractive—and that he'd like to follow it up. And that by offering her that marvellous room, he'd practically staked a claim on her.

Men! Her mother was right—they only had one object in view where women were concerned, and that was a sex object. Maybe some women liked that kind of thing and were willing to go along with it—but she wasn't. As she'd told Marc, she valued her self-respect too much to fall into bed with every personable man who happened to come along. And as it happened, Kurt Brunner wasn't the kind of man she'd go for anyway—too smooth, too handsome, with that sleek blond head, those sky-blue eyes, those regular features and perfect teeth. Too perfect altogether—and Jan distrusted perfection. There had to be a flaw somewhere, and she preferred to be able to see them. Flaws like a cragginess of feature that broke up the perfect symmetry yet hinted at inner strength, flaws like teeth that were slightly irregular, giving an odd charm to a crooked smile, and telling of a lack of vanity, quirky humour. Flaws like a sudden, irascible temper, a tendency to demand impossibly high standards from himself and everyone else, so that all those who worked for him were stretched to their limits, forced to reach a potential they'd never thought they had. . .

Jan jerked her mind away from the picture conjured up in her mind and thought instead of the corner Marc Tyrell had driven her into. If he hadn't come bursting in just at that moment yesterday afternoon, she'd have refused that sumptuous room and asked for the broom-cupboard instead. But Marc's attitude had infuriated her and she'd taken the room just as an act of defiance, landing herself in a position as difficult as any she'd ever been in. Kurt Brunner was complacently sure that she was his for the taking—a ripe plum, just begging to be picked. And just at this moment, she didn't have any idea how to tell him otherwise.

And it was all Marc's fault—damn him! *Damn* him!

She was almost relieved to hear the door open and look up to see Marc standing frowning at the entrance to the lounge.

'Ah,' said Kurt, rising to his feet with the easy grace she had already noticed in him. 'Here is Mr Tyrell. A cocktail for you too, Mr Tyrell? Jan is enjoying hers, I think.'

Marc gave him a dark, sweeping glance. 'A cocktail? I think not, thank you. I prefer something a little plainer. Perhaps a whisky, if you have such a thing.'

'But of course.' Kurt went to the bar in the corner of the room, and Marc sat down next to Jan and turned his head to look at her. She met his gaze steadily for a moment, then felt a flush colour her cheeks and turned away to pick up her drink.

'You ought to try this,' she said, conscious that her voice was higher than usual. 'It's Kurt's own blend—quite delicious.'

'Looks like a fruit salad to me,' he said dismissively. 'Never did like drinks I had to chew. Sure it won't spoil your dinner, as Nanny used to say?'

Jan threw him a withering glance and sipped from the tall glass. There was rather a lot of fruit in it, bumping against her lips, but she wasn't going to admit to Marc that she'd really rather have had a plain Martini. She set the glass down again and gave Kurt an appreciative smile as he came back with Marc's whisky.

'That's a wonderful drink, Kurt. Does it have a name?'

The sky-blue eyes smiled at her. 'Until now, it has been called Jungfrau Sunset—but now I think I shall give it a new name. Simply—Jan.' The white teeth flashed and Jan heard a muffled snort from beside her. For a moment, she was in danger of dissolving into giggles herself—but the thought of Marc's jeering if she did saved her. Instead, she let her twitching lips smile at Kurt and said, 'Thank you. That's very nice—isn't it, Marc?' She nudged him sharply. 'Did you hear? Kurt's named his cocktail after me. I don't believe I've ever had a cocktail named after me before.'

'Really?' Marc said weakly, and caught her eye. 'Well, that's—charming.' She could see that he was about to collapse again and gave him a quick, surreptitious kick on the ankle. 'Do you know, I don't believe I've ever had one called after me either.' He lifted his own glass and buried his face in it.

Jan turned away in exasperation. Who would have thought the lofty Marc Tyrell capable of giving way to a sense of the ridiculous? It didn't help that she'd been equally struck by the desire to laugh at the contrast between the romantic floweriness of Jungfrau Sunset and her own short, plain name. But she would never have dreamed of hurting Kurt's feelings by doing so. He might have thought she was laughing at him, and that certainly wouldn't have been true.

She sought for something to say, but before she could open her mouth the door opened and Kurt turned to see who was coming in. And at the expression on his face, Jan turned as well. And forgot all about cocktails.

The woman who stood in the doorway was magnificent. There was no other word for her. Tall, statuesque, with hair of a deep blonde that shimmered to bare shoulders exquisitely set off by a low-cut gown of moonshadow-blue velvet, she would have drawn all eyes wherever she went. Her eyes were as dark as her dress, subtly shadowed and outlined, her lips full and red, held in a slight pout. Blonde as she was, there was a sultriness about her that even Jan could recognise as blatant sex appeal, and she was conscious of Marc's sitting upright in the chair beside her.

'*Renate!*' said Kurt, on a whisper.

The woman moved forward out of the shadow. Her gown was full-length, and rippled like a cascade of deep blue water as she glided across the carpet, pooling around her silver shoes. She was smiling and holding out her hands, and Kurt, like a man mesmerised, went to take them in his.

'Renate—I didn't know you were coming. You didn't let me know.' He spoke rapidly in German and she answered him, laughing. Then he looked down at Jan and spoke again in English. 'I must apologise—we are acting impolitely. Renate, these are two English guests at the hotel, from the British television, so interesting, we must all have a long talk together. . . Miss Jan Cartwright, Mr Marc Tyrell. . . And this is my cousin Renate, who follows me everywhere, but didn't tell me she was coming to Mürren today, so she is a naughty girl, *nicht wahr*?' He shook her hands chidingly, but his face was beaming with pleasure. 'For penance, Renate, you must sit down at once and drink one of my cocktails, and I must tell you at once that I have just renamed it Jan, in Miss Cartwright's honour.'

'But how delicious!' The Swiss woman sank gracefully into the chair beside Marc and looked past him at Jan. 'You must have made a very good impression on my cousin, Miss Cartwright. He is about his cocktails very particular.'

Jan smiled but said nothing. Looking sideways, she could see that Marc was leaning back again in his chair, cradling his glass in his hands. He was watching Renate with a curious expression on his face, and Jan realised again just how beautiful Kurt's cousin was.

'And so what are you doing in Switzerland?' the husky voice enquired. 'For the climbing, have you come? Or the walking through our beautiful flower-meadows? The alpenrose is at its best now—perhaps you like the photographs to take?'

'Well, in a way,' Marc answered in the slow, lazy voice he used when he was relaxed. He sent her a smile that Jan thought would have turned her heart over if she had been on the receiving end. Thank goodness she wasn't. . . 'We're here to reconnoitre for a TV programme about famous fictional detectives. Do you happen to know anything about that kind of thing?'

'I?' Renate gave a low, throaty chuckle. 'I never open a book! But Kurt reads a great deal—I'm sure he'll be able to help you. Have you not asked him already?' She looked up as Kurt returned to them with a tall glass for her and a jug from which he topped up Jan's cocktail. 'You read detective fiction, Kurt, *nicht wahr*——?'

'Do you, Kurt?' Jan cut in quickly with her brightest smile. 'If so, you could be an enormous help to us—I'm sure you must know quite a lot about how this area was used by people like Fleming and Conan Doyle.' She flashed a second smile at Marc, ignoring the glower he sent back to her. 'Don't you?'

'But of course—who does not?' Kurt offered Marc the whisky and received a mutter of thanks. 'Even those who don't read at all cannot fail to have seen the Bond

films or to have heard of the famous Sherlock Holmes.
And here in Switzerland. . .' His eyes sharpened. 'You
will be visiting our Reichenbach Falls, without doubt?
Perhaps spending a little time in Meiringen?'

'Oh yes, we intend to include those in our filming,'
Jan said before Marc could answer. 'In fact, we're going
on there after we finish here, aren't we, Marc?'

'Then you must do me the honour of staying at the
hotel I have there,' Kurt declared, and smiled at Jan's
obvious surprise. 'Yes, it is true—the Sonnschein is not
the only hotel I own. In fact, I have several. But the one
at Meiringen is special.' He smiled. 'It is a *Schloss*, you
see—a castle, set high among woodland and overlooking
a small lake, above the town itself and not very far from
the Falls. It is quite certain, I think, that Conan Doyle
would have seen it, possibly even visited it. You would
be moving in an environment that he might well have
known himself; you might even use it for your filming,
for background and atmosphere if nothing else.'

'Oh, I don't think so,' Jan said quickly. Stay at Kurt's
Schloss, where she'd be under even more of an obligation
to him than she was here? 'It sounds wonderful, of
course, but we're already booked in at a hotel in the
town.' She turned to Marc for confirmation. 'That's
right, isn't it? And the budget——'

'But you would be my guests, *natürlich*,' Kurt said.
'As if I would expect anything else! And Renate will be
there too, won't you?' He smiled at his cousin.

'Without doubt,' she said, and gave Marc a long look
from her deep blue eyes. 'I love the *Schloss* like a second
home. I always spend the summer there.' She kept her
eyes on Marc's. 'Do come!'

'Really?' Jan said faintly. 'Well, I'm afraid it's out of
the question, isn't it, Marc?'

But to her astonishment, Marc was looking at Renate with a strange mixture of interest and speculation, as if wondering. . . But what could he be wondering? she asked herself impatiently. He'd only just met the woman, for heaven's sake. And wasn't likely to meet her again—unless they did go to stay at this *Schloss*. And he surely couldn't be intending. . .

'It's out of the question, isn't it?' she repeated sharply.

Marc turned and looked at her. He was smiling, a secret, enigmatic smile that made her want to shake him. She stared at him, willing him to answer her.

'A *Schloss*, hm?' he said at last. 'Sounds interesting. Very interesting. As you say, we could do some filming there—for one of the other episodes, if not this one. Does a *Schloss* come into any other detective story, Jan? You might do some research on that.'

'But what about the hotel booking we've already made? The other hotel——'

He flicked his fingers impatiently. 'We can cancel that. We're not due there for nearly a week—they'll soon fill the rooms. And if not, it won't cost the budget any more to pay for our rooms.' He turned back to Kurt. 'We'd be very grateful to take you up on your offer, Kurt. Thanks a lot.'

'But——' Jan turned from one to the other, desperately searching for words. 'Kurt, I really don't think—Marc, we *can't*! Everything's arranged—I fixed it all up——'

'So unfix it,' he said, lying back in his chair, his dark head unnervingly close to Renate's gleaming blonde hair. 'One thing you've got to be in this business, Jan, is flexible. Haven't you learnt that yet?'

She stared at him, fury and indignation seething inside her. *Flexible?* Was that what he called it—this abrupt

change of attitude that could take him from outright
hostility towards Kurt to easy acceptance of his hospitality? Half an hour ago, he'd been ready to believe
anything of the Swiss hotelier—yes, and anything of her
too, simply because she'd accepted a better room in this
hotel. Now he was proposing to go along with a free
week for both of them in what must be even more
expensive accommodation—and why? What could possibly have changed his mind?

There was only one answer to that. Renate. The
glamorous Swiss woman who was beside him now,
laughing softly at something he'd said, leaning close to
him so that he could receive the full benefit of that
voluptuously swelling figure. . .

Jan turned away, disgust warring with something more
painful, turning a knife in her heart. And caught Kurt's
eye, watching her with an expression that was easy to
understand.

Well, at least Marc might be too occupied now to
criticise her every action. And if he dared, she would be
able to come right back at him with that old proverb
about pots calling kettles black!

It was not until after dinner, when they were alone in
the lounge, that she was able to give vent at last to her
feelings. Kurt and Renate had disappeared to his private
apartment—'to exchange family news', Renate had
smiled as they went—the other guests had left and the
lounge was empty; even the girl behind the bar had
disappeared. Jan stared angrily out of the window,
waiting for Marc to speak. At last, she turned on him.

'And just what was all that about? Why are you so
keen all of a sudden to stay at this *Schloss* of Kurt's?
After all you've said about my taking that room
upstairs——'

'What does that have to do with it?' he asked. 'It's completely different——'

'*Different?*'

'Of course it is. What's so wrong with staying at Kurt's *Schloss*? Are we supposed to be looking for local colour or not? And it's not going to involve us in any extra expense—in fact, it'll cost nothing at all. He's invited us as his *guests*—and he doesn't just mean hotel guests.'

'I know that. And that's what worries me.' Jan's eyes were unhappy as she looked at him. 'Why should he want to do that, Marc? He's only known us a couple of days. Why would he offer us his hospitality at what must be an expensive hotel?'

'Can't you guess?' asked Marc in an amused tone.

She swung her body away from his in the big armchair. 'Oh, for goodness' sake give it a rest, Marc! You've got an obsession about Kurt and his supposed designs on me. Can't your mind run on any track other than sex?' She tried to dismiss the uncomfortable thought that Marc might just be right. 'What man would tie up two rooms in his hotel just on the chance of a bit of—of——'

'Of what, Jan? Don't you like saying the words? Or don't you know them?' An infuriating smile played around Marc's lips, then he sat up straight and fixed her with a glance of steel. 'Now listen to me. It isn't *my* mind that keeps running on sex. As it happens, I *don't* think that's why Kurt's asked us to his hotel, or I wouldn't go within a mile of the place. I've already told you, I don't want. my researcher distracted. And now that I've seen Renate I'm quite happy on that score——'

'Renate? She's his cousin!'

'So? Only a second or third cousin, she tells me—the relationship is really quite distant. Anyway, the point is that Kurt's quite obviously tied up with her, so you're safe.' He ignored Jan's gasp of indignation. 'As for Kurt's real purpose in offering us hospitality, it's childishly simple to understand. He *wants* us to see his hotel, Jan. We're TV people—we could bring him a lot of business. We might use it to film ourselves, or we might go home and tell other TV people—holiday programmes, other film-makers, anyone. Look, he's not offering us anything for free—he hopes to get business from our visit. *Now* do you understand?'

Jan looked mutely at him. Put like that, it did sound quite feasible. People did offer their homes or their hotels for TV filming, and make quite respectable sums of money from it. It might indeed be all that Kurt had in mind.

All the same. . .she remembered the look on Kurt's face as he'd watched her, and wasn't so sure. And she wasn't sure either that Marc was right about him and Renate—they hadn't behaved like lovers. Just as cousins. And from the way Renate had looked at Marc— and the way he'd looked at her. . .

With another pang, Jan realised that, although Marc might well be right about Kurt's reasons for inviting them to the *Schloss*, he hadn't fully explained his own for accepting. All right, so it could be useful for local colour—but was that really all?

'So you don't care if all this puts me into a difficult position?' she asked in a small voice. 'You don't care if Kurt puts a somewhat different interpretation on my presence at his hotel?'

Marc threw her a glance so scornful that she shrivelled inside. 'You? In a difficult position? Come off it, Jan!

Any difficulties you might be in are entirely of your own making. You've already made sure of that here—going to the *Schloss* isn't going to make a scrap of difference to that.' He eyed her appraisingly. 'In fact, this just gives you a chance to prove that professionalism of yours you're so proud of.'

'And how do I do that?' she demanded.

'Why, by simply going along with this arrangement. Accepting Kurt's invitation purely on a professional level and keeping it that way. By not even admitting that he might have an ulterior motive. By not even letting it into your mind.' His glance became a challenge. 'If you don't want men's minds running continually on sex, you mustn't let yours run on it either. Treat him as you want to be treated—as a person. Isn't that the truly professional way to go about it? The truly *equal* way?'

Jan was silent. She could find no answer to Marc's words. She had to admit that he was right.

'All right,' she said at last, 'I'll do that. But if it doesn't work—if he still thinks——'

'He'll think whatever you let him think,' Marc stated. 'It's up to you, Jan—entirely up to you. You're the liberated woman around here.'

He turned away from her and looked out of the window. And Jan, her mind still busy with his words, followed his gaze.

The sun was low now and a flush of apricot was spreading over the blue dome of the sky. The colour had just begun to touch the shimmering white peaks; as she watched, it spread over them, flushing the gleaming slopes to a faint, pearly rose which deepened to glowing coral. Jan caught her breath. In the face of such beauty, her quarrel with Marc seemed shabby, cheapened to an ill-tempered squabble between tired children. She felt the tears sting her eyes and longed suddenly to share all this with someone whose heart was in accord with her own.

A light touch on her hand brought her eyes from the vastness outside. She looked down and saw Marc's fingers resting on hers. Raising her eyes, she saw a look on his face such as she had never seen before; a tenderness that he had kept hidden from her, an awareness that seemed to speak directly to her soul.

'Let's not spoil this,' he said quietly. 'I know we don't agree, Jan—on many things. But we're one when we watch the light on the mountains. Let's forget everything else but this—just for now. All right?'

She looked into his eyes, softened now by the warm light of the sunset, and nodded. He was right. Tomorrow, they would disagree again, about almost everything. They would argue and struggle and fight until they had reached some conclusion, until they had made a programme that would satisfy them both. That was why Lucia had sent them here, because she knew that out of their discord would come harmony. Not a personal harmony, but the professional harmony she needed for her job.

But for now, they were together in their worship of the mountains. And as they sat there, watching, Jan relaxed beside the man who normally roused every antagonistic fibre in her, and left her hand in his. For now, it made the moment complete.

CHAPTER FIVE

'WELL, that seems to be pretty well tied up.' Marc leaned back in his chair, stretching his long arms above his head. 'We use the clips from *OHMSS* and our own filming of what Piz Gloria is really like. Plus a few nice shots of the village and general surroundings, for atmosphere. Should go down well. I reckon that's all we can do here, for the time being. Leave tomorrow, OK?'

'Yes, I suppose so.' Jan cast a wistful glance at the big window, taking in the last of the view of the mountains before the alpenglow faded and night threw a blanket of shadows over the shivering peaks. 'I must admit I'll miss this room—though Kurt's promised one just as good at the *Schloss*.' Then she frowned. She still didn't like the idea of accepting Kurt's offer of rooms at his other hotel, but, after what had amounted to a challenge to her professionalism from Marc, she'd been unable to find any sound reason for refusing—even though she strongly suspected that Kurt wouldn't even begin to understand her ideals. But he *hadn't* made any passes at her while they were here, after all. And presumably he wouldn't even be around at the *Schloss*, so, as Marc said, where was the problem? And, since they would almost certainly also take advantage of his offer to film there, it would have been not only unprofessional but childish to reject the Swiss hotelier's hospitality—although she was pretty sure that it was Renate's presence rather than the offer of filming there that had persuaded Marc it was a good idea.

And that was a thought that was peculiarly unwelcome.

She rose briskly from her chair and began to shuffle their papers together. 'Well, let's get tidied up and have a drink.' She had grown accustomed to Marc's presence in her room now, accepting the sense of using it as a private sitting-room for the two of them to have their discussions, and it had become a routine to finish their work with a drink together. Since the day they had had lunch at the Piz Gloria restaurant and Marc had been so blunt with her they had shared an uneasy truce. Provided they stuck to work, everything was fine—it was when they allowed personal topics to creep in that the fur began to fly.

Now, as she went over to the small bar cupboard, Jan wondered if Kurt would be joining them as he had promised. She looked out at the mountains, now little more than looming shadows in the dusk, and sighed.

'What's the trouble?' Marc asked quietly. 'Sorry to be leaving?'

'Yes, I am, rather.' Jan came back to the table with a tray of glasses and bottles. 'It's so beautiful here, so peaceful. I feel I could spend the rest of my life here quite happily—forget the rat race of life outside and settle down——'

'To being a hotelier's wife, no doubt.' Marc's tone hardened and Jan saw that he was looking at the tray. Thinking of Kurt, she had set out three glasses. 'I take it lover-boy's joining us.'

'Marc, I've told you, he is *not* my lover!'

'But you wish he were, or I'm very much mistaken. Oh, I know what you *say*—all this protesting about staying at the *Schloss*—but you don't fool me. I've seen the way he looks at you, yes, and the way you play up to him too—fluttering your eyelashes, stroking back your hair, all the little tricks.' His lips curled sardonically as Jan's colour deepened. 'Well——' he got to his feet '—far be it from me to interfere in love's young dream on the eve of parting. I'll forgo that drink, Jan. You can put one of the glasses away.'

Jan straightened and faced him. Her heart was thumping hard and her breast was tight with anger. Steel-grey eyes met her own and she did not trouble to hide her bitterness as she spoke.

'Marc, I've had just about enough of this! Ever since we came here, I've had nothing but innuendoes from you about me, about Kurt, about what we do together. Over and over again, I've told you we do *nothing*. When would we have time? But you refuse to believe that, don't you? You refuse to believe that any woman could be with an attractive man for five minutes without falling into bed with him. Just what is it with you, Marc Tyrell? Just what makes you see women in that disgusting, degrading way? Why can't you see that we're normal human beings, with normal desires, yes, but with the ability to control them—even if we *do* feel attracted? Doesn't it ever occur to you that we do discriminate— that sex doesn't invariably come first anyway? That we might think more of our careers and all the other facets of life—and there are many, Marc, many—and that some of us might even prefer to do without the delights of male dominance so that we can just get on and lead our lives the way *we* want to? Or don't you think at all. Maybe you're so hidebound and riddled with old-fashioned ideas that you've never even tried—you've just accepted all the old clichés as a package, to save yourself the trouble!'

She panted into silence and they stared at each other.

Marc looked down into her face without expression. Then something flickered in his eyes and was gone. His mouth twitched and, to Jan's fury, she saw that he was smiling.

'Well, we are the little spitfire, aren't we?' he said evenly. 'Quite an impassioned speech—I congratulate you. There's even more of your mother in you than I thought.'

'My mother?' Jan echoed stupidly. 'What do you know of my mother? You told me you'd never met her——'

'I know what the rest of the world knows. That she's one of the most militant feminists since Germaine Greer—that she holds men in utter contempt and never loses an opportunity to say so. That she's beaten her unfortunate husband into abject submission and——'

'Stop it! How *dare* you?' Jan raised her hand to strike his face, but he lifted a hand and caught her wrist easily in his. 'Let me *go*!'

'Not while you're offering physical violence. It solves nothing.' His voice was cool and implacable, his fingers like iron. She hesitated, angrily aware of his greater strength, then subsided. Marc let her go and she rubbed her wrist, glaring at him with venom.

'All right, so maybe you think that's a bit strong. But you ought to know it, Jan. You ought to know what people say about your parents, about your mother in particular. She isn't liked, you know. And he—well, I'm sorry to say it, but he's both pitied and despised. OK——' he lifted a hand again, warding off her increasing anger '—I know it's not nice to hear that about your own parents. But you must have realised—she's a media person herself, you can't be unaware of the antagonism she stirs up.'

'Of course I'm not. But that's from people who are uninformed—unenlightened—or who have their own stake in the subject. It's nothing personal. And Daddy——'

'Don't say he has nothing to do with it,' Marc advised her. 'It just isn't true, you know.'

'But it is! He keeps right away from my mother's work. He has his own interests——'

'Like shutting himself up in his study. Living in his own ivory tower, his hermit's cave if you like. Like letting her go her own way, never lifting a finger to stop her from her excesses.'

'Daddy *believes* in what my mother does,' Jan declared, but Marc shook his head.

'That's not the way I understand it. Jan, I've met your father. Maybe he's never mentioned this, but I was one of his students, a long time ago. And we've kept in touch since. We don't meet very often, but when we do, we talk. And I know quite a lot about his life—more, probably, than he thinks he's told me.'

Jan felt her face whiten. 'Just what are you saying?' she whispered.

He reached out and took her hands in his. He drew her back to the armchairs and sat her down, then drew the second chair nearer to it. Their knees almost touched as he also sat down, leaning forward. In the almost dark room, she could just see the pale oval of his face, the gleam of his eyes and teeth.

'Jan, that's no marriage, what he has with your mother. It's a travesty, and he knows it. He's endured it for one reason only—for you. Because he couldn't quite bear to go off and leave you entirely in her care. He's always felt that there must be something he could do, some day, to help you.'

'To help me? But I don't need help!'

'Your father thinks you do,' Marc said quietly. 'And so do I, Jan. You're in danger of ruining your own life, just as your mother's ruined hers.'

'My *mother's* life—ruined? You're crazy! She's completely absorbed in her work—where's the ruin in that?'

'Is she happy, Jan?' He waited a moment. 'I'd say not. From what I've seen of your mother, she's a bitter, resentful and unhappy woman. She's eaten up with twisted ideas about half the human race—the male half. She can't see that the two sexes can be complementary in all the best senses of the word. She's driven your father into almost complete seclusion and she's imbuing you with the same distorted ideas.'

There was silence. Then Jan said, her voice dry and painful, 'You're going too far, Marc.'

'Am I?' He shook his head. 'I think not, Jan. In fact, I'm probably not going far enough. It's time you saw the truth—started to think for yourself.'

'I do think for myself!' Uncomfortably, she recalled the questions she had begun to ask during the past few months, the questions that had made her feel disloyal to her mother and her ideals, but which had refused to go away unanswered. Quickly, she pulled her mind away from them and tried another line of attack. 'I'm surprised you asked for me as your researcher, since you obviously think I'm nothing but a mouthpiece for my mother,' she said caustically.

But Marc shook his head. 'Not at all. I've watched you work with other directors and I believe you've got something extra—something you put into the programmes you work on. But you're going to lose it, Jan, if you don't get your own thinking sorted out.' He paused and then went on, 'And I'm not prepared to sit back and let that happen. I'm not like your father, Jan. I'm prepared to fight for what I value.'

His hands were on hers again, gripping tightly. She felt the fire leap from his fingers into her own palms, spreading up her arms and into her breasts. She looked down at the hands, almost invisible in the gathering darkness, and tried to withdraw, but his grip was too firm.

'I—I don't understand.'

'You're a little fool at times, Jan Cartwright,' Marc muttered, and his voice was deep now, deep with a husky note she had never heard in it before. 'You're infuriating, bigoted, argumentative and obstinate, and heaven knows why I bother with you. But somehow you've got under my skin and I'm damned if I'll let you go the same way as that virago of a mother of yours. . . Damned if I will!'

With a sudden movement he jerked her from her seat and into his arms. Taken completely by surprise, she fell upon him as he lay back in his chair and found herself clasped firmly against his body, her mouth claimed in a kiss that drove all the breath from her. For a moment she struggled; then the kiss, with all its probing, demanding passion, drove every thought from her mind and she gave a tiny moan and relaxed against him, pressing herself down on his hard, splayed body, letting her mouth soften against his.

'Lord. . .' he muttered, and she felt his hands move urgently over her. 'Oh, lord. . .Jan, Jan, Jan. . .'

There was a tiny moment of pause and then he twisted her underneath him, so that they lay close together in the big armchair. She could feel his breath, warm on her cheek, as his mouth explored her hair, her eyelids, her ears and neck. There was a tingling in her breasts and she could feel the swelling hardness, the tautness of her nipples as they strained against the thin blouse she wore. Already, his fingers were at the buttons, letting them loose, letting the full breasts, covered only by a wisp of lace, spill into his hands. His lips once again on hers, he cupped the fullness in his palms and then tore his mouth away and bent to lay it against the rosy tips.

Jan lay quiescent, scarcely able to believe what was happening. Was this really Marc Tyrell, the tough, ruthless director, the man who suffered no fool gladly or even at all, the man who had treated her with contempt, who had accused her of wantonness and said unforgivable things about her parents? What was she doing, lying here and allowing him to touch her body in this way, to kiss her like this, to rouse her blood to such a thundering roar, her body to such frantic desire? Yet she had no wish to prevent him now; she only wanted him to go on, to use her as he liked, to take her and make her his. . .the first man she had ever loved, the only man. . .

Love? What was she thinking of? She didn't love this man—she couldn't! It was lust, that was all, the desire of one human body for another. It meant nothing. It couldn't possibly mean anything.

Jan twisted herself away from his hands, jerked her body out of the chair. Dragging her blouse together, she stared down at him, seeing in the light of the rising moon the astonishment on his face.

'Get out of here!' she panted, backing away towards the window. 'Get out! Get *out*!'

Marc scrambled to his feet. 'Jan! Jan, what is it? What's the matter?'

'Don't even ask me that!' She turned away, letting all her self-disgust flood into her voice. 'Just get out and don't ever try that again!'

He stared at her, his eyes narrowed. 'What in hell's that supposed to mean? I got the distinct impression that you were all for it——'

'Then you were wrong!' she snapped. 'Oh, you're very expert—I'll give you that. Maybe most girls do respond to your attentions—but I'm not one of them, understand? I happen to be able to use my brain, even while you're trying to use my body. . .' A fresh sensation of desire wafted over her as the memory of just how his hands and lips had felt came flooding back into her mind. She quivered, but with an effort took hold of herself again. Any more of that and she'd be back in his arms, and she wasn't going to let that happen. 'Just go away,' she added tiredly. 'Please.'

But Marc seemed to have no intention of going away. He stood still, massive and immovable as a rock, his eyes glowering now in the dim, shifting light. Slowly he raised a hand, and Jan flinched. But he was merely passing it back over his dark, tousled hair, as if bewildered. Bewildered indeed! she thought contemptuously. He knew damned well what she meant.

He spoke again, his voice grim.

'Now look here, Jan. I'll admit I didn't intend that to happen—I came here tonight to talk, to try to make you see reason. I've told you, you're in danger of making a big mistake, and that matters to me, believe it or not.' He sighed. 'Goodness knows why! I'm not even sure *I* believe it at times, but it's true. I just don't want to see you. . .' He threw her a quick glance. 'Well, never mind that. The fact is, there's something between us that can't be ignored. *You* can't ignore it and I'm damned sure I can't. We've been aching for each other ever since that first day in my office—well, haven't we?' He lifted a hand as Jan began to speak. 'Don't bother to deny it,

Jan—I'm not a novice in these matters, though I'm not the womaniser you seem to think. There's only been one woman who mattered in my life before now, and she decided she preferred her career and went to America. . . And even with her, I never felt. . .Look, Jan, I don't know what this all means. Love—lust—chemistry— whatever name you like to give it, it's there between us and it won't go away. So why not just give in and enjoy it, without worrying too much about what it'll lead to?'

Jan looked at him with contempt.

'That's just the kind of suggestion I'd expect from you,' she said coldly. 'And I'm afraid it's not on. You talk about *me* making mistakes—well, you're the one who's making them now. Chemistry—you talk as if I'm some kind of experiment. You talk as if we're *making* some kind of experiment! Well, I'm sorry, but I'm not interested. I don't imagine any experiment we could carry out together would be likely to lead to anything.' She gave him a scathing glance. 'You know what your trouble really is? You're jealous—jealous of Kurt. Because he's everything you're not.'

'Oh, for crying out loud! Jealous of that knitting pattern?' Marc made a swift movement of scorn. 'Jan, you have to be joking!'

'I'm not, and you *are* jealous,' she repeated stubbornly. 'Because he knows how to treat a woman, and you don't——'

'For heaven's sake! He treats you just as I always thought you feminists didn't *want* to be treated! Opening doors—lifting you down off trains—running around after you as if you were some precious piece of porcelain! Isn't that exactly what you've fought so much against? Isn't it what you've always believed demeans you?'

'In a way, yes.' Jan tried not to betray her own

uneasiness. She didn't really enjoy Kurt's attentive-
ness—she'd only encouraged it in the first place to annoy
Marc, and had been alarmed by the way it had got out
of hand—first this room, then the *Schloss*. All the same,
she still wasn't going to let Marc know how uncomfortable it made her to be continually fussed over and treated
like a fragile piece of glass. 'But he does it because it
comes *naturally* to him to behave that way. He genuinely
believes in it. You—and all the other men I've ever
met—you do it to ingratiate yourselves. Because you're
hoping to impress—because you're out to get something
from it.'

'And Kurt's not?'

'No,' she said, 'I don't believe he is.' She gave Marc a
proud look. 'He's not made the slightest pass at me.'

'Then there's something seriously wrong with him!'
Marc said brutally. 'And something wrong with you too,
that you can't see it. Jan, it isn't natural for a man to
behave that way round a pretty, unattached woman.
There has to be some reason. . . And you must surely
realise it yourself deep down.' He studied her for a
moment. 'Or does it just make you feel safe? Safe from
the real emotions you're so terrified of betraying?'

'I don't know what you mean——' Jan began angrily,
but he shook his head.

'I think you do, Jan. You've been so brainwashed into
thinking men are a positive threat to you that you're
scared of any man who shows a normal healthy interest
in you. You're just plain frightened, Jan. And Kurt
Brunner, who pays all the so-called proper attentions to
you, without ever doing anything to scare that bewildered little girl inside you, makes you feel safe.' He
shook his head again. 'Whereas when you get a *real*
man. . .well, we both know now, don't we, Jan, that

there's a real woman in there, struggling like crazy to get out?'

She stared at him for a moment, then looked away. Her heart was thumping, her cheeks were burning and she felt sick.

'I think you've said enough now, Marc,' she said at last, her voice low. 'All right, I'm sorry if you think I led you on—that's what men always say, isn't it? But I certainly never intended to and it'll never happen again. I'll make sure of that. And now—go away. Or do I have to ring for room service?'

'No, you don't have to do that.' He rose to his feet, staring at her in the pale light now flooding into the room. 'I don't suppose you know the German word for "bouncer" anyway. All right, Jan, I'll go. I'll leave you to whatever dreams you prefer. Or maybe the Swiss Casanova will be along to soothe your indignant breast. It's certain sure I won't be trying again!' He moved towards the door, then paused and looked back. 'I can see why your father's so worried about you,' he said coldly. 'Only trouble is, he's left it a bit late. You've gone beyond redemption, Jan. You're your mother's daughter, through and through, and there's not a thing that can be done to change you.'

After Marc had gone, Jan sat for a long time in the big armchair which had so recently held their two bodies. She stared out of the window at the mountains, lit now by an unearthly light, at the deep blue shadows lying like wounds between the ebony crags, and she thought painfully over all that Marc had said and done.

Her first reaction was of anger, a blind, trembling fury that gripped and possessed her so that she could do nothing but shake and whisper over and over again,

'How dare he—how *dare* he?' To speak of her mother in
that way—how could he even think that she would listen
for one moment to such slander? Eaten up with resent-
ment—bitter, unhappy—full of twisted ideas—her
mother? Susan Cartwright, known for her strong opinions and the power she possessed to express them? Susan
Cartwright, whose articles appeared in all the most
modern magazines, who spoke regularly on the radio,
whose face was familiar to TV viewers through debate
and opinion programmes? No, it wasn't Jan's mother
who was bitter and twisted, it was Marc Tyrell—eaten
up with jealousy and bitterness of his own, and using it
as a weapon to injure her.

And her father—yes, it was true, he lived his own
quiet life, apart from most of his wife's doings. But that
was simply because he believed in her—because he
agreed that husbands and wives should not have to live
in each other's pockets but could go their own way.
But—beaten into submission? Pitied and despised?
Deeply unhappy?

He wasn't any of those things. He couldn't be.

Could he?

Jan stirred then and leaned forward, sinking her head
into her hands. Fight it as she might, she couldn't stop
those words circling in her brain, torturing her with the
possibility that Marc might have seen what she had been
blind to. If it was true that he knew her father—and that
must be so, it could so easily be checked—then it might
also be true that Professor Cartwright had talked with
him. Had confided in him.

But if so, why hadn't her father mentioned that he
knew Marc Tyrell? Or had he? Hadn't he murmured
something about knowing him, something that her
mother had swept aside? Jan tried to remember, then

gave up. In any case, she still couldn't believe that he would have said those things.

Marc Tyrell was lying—and he was lying either to hurt her, or to gain power over her.

Because his ego had been bruised; because she preferred Kurt Brunner to him.

As Kurt's name came into her mind, Jan heard a sound at the door. She turned quickly, her heart kicking. If it was Marc, come back. . . But the figure standing in the shaft of moonlight that streamed across the big room was not that of Marc Tyrell. It was Kurt himself, his corn-gold hair turned to silver, his eyes gleaming brightly, the flash of his teeth echoing the brilliance of the mountains outside. Oh, no!

'Kurt. . .' She began.

'Did you think I would not come? On your last night here?' He crossed the room swiftly. 'But why are you sitting like this, in the dark? Are you admiring the moonlight on our beautiful mountains?'

'Yes—yes, I am.' She was thankful that he did not immediately snap on the light but instead dropped to his knees beside her, looking out.

'*Wunderbar*!' he murmured. 'Where else will you find such a view—such exquisite beauty? And you, Jan, you feel it as I do, *nicht wahr*? It speaks to your heart as it speaks to mine. The moonlight on the snow—the magnificence of the peaks—ah, there can be nothing finer in the whole of the world!'

'No,' she said, finding her voice, 'nothing.' Her mind was whirling. How was she going to handle this? After accepting so much, how was she going to refuse him what he so clearly expected? Oh God, what a fool she'd been! Marc had been right—she ought to have insisted on the broom-cupboard. And if she hadn't been so stupidly intent on annoying him, she wouldn't be in this position now. She sought desperately for the right words.

Kurt turned and looked searchingly into her face. 'Jan? There is something wrong? Your voice—you sound upset. Something has happened? Tell me!'

His voice was suddenly commanding, but his hands, taking hers, were gentle. She shook her head. Play it cool, that was the only way.

'No, nothing has happened. I'm just sad to be leaving here. It's been such a short time. . .'

'Too short,' he declared. 'And we have seen so little of each other. A dinner here and there—a drink—it is not enough. No, if you were not going on to the *Schloss*, I would certainly not let you go so soon. But there, we shall have more time to be together. I have arranged it!'

Jan stared at him. 'Arranged it? But—how? Surely you'll be here?'

'And why? When the *Schloss* is mine as well? Do you think I never go to see it, to make my presence felt? I have an admirable manager there, it is true—but I spend much time there myself. After all, it is my home, the home of my childhood, I have a great fondness——'

'Your *home*? You mean you grew up there?'

'But of course. I was born there. It has been my family home for generations. Have I not said?'

Jan shook her head bemusedly. A castle! No wonder Kurt was so self-possessed, so sure of himself. His family must have been one of the aristocratic dynasties of the country. Yet Brunner was such a common name. . .

'I never use my family name, of course,' he remarked, reading her mind. 'Not for my business. I prefer Brunner—a good, solid Swiss name. But that is not important now. Jan. . .' his hands tightened around hers '. . .I want to talk to you. There are things I must say. . .I had intended to keep them until we were at the *Schloss*, but tonight is so beautiful—I feel I cannot let this moment go.' His eyes were on hers, his face lit by the brilliance of the moon. 'Jan, I have never met a woman like you. You have done something to me which no other woman has ever achieved. You have taken my heart. It is in your hands, to keep or to destroy. Do you understand what I am trying to say?'

Jan could feel the tension in his fingers as they clasped her wrists; his voice vibrated with an intensity that alarmed her. Her body trembling, she tried to draw away, but Kurt's hands tightened further and he came nearer, his body close to hers, his mouth almost touching her cheek.

'Since you came to Mürren, Jan, I have not been the same man,' he said in a low, throbbing voice. 'As soon as I saw you on that train, I knew—here was my woman, the one I have waited for. Here is the girl of my dreams, the lover of my heart. Can you tell me, truly, that you have not felt this too? That you have not felt drawn to me?'

'Kurt——' she began helplessly. 'I——'

'Don't answer at once,' he said quickly. 'I know you Englishwomen—you are shy, you need time. And I will give you that time. Because I know that one day, quite soon, you will turn to me and offer your heart in exchange for mine. This I know without any doubt.'

Jan closed her eyes. Still emotionally bruised from her encounter with Marc, she knew this was a situation she really didn't need. She felt him release her hands and take her gently into his arms.

'Marc Tyrell is not the man for you,' he murmured against her hair. 'You know that already, don't you?

Even though, when he looks at you sometimes, his heart is in his eyes. But he——'

'Oh, no, that's not true! Marc doesn't care for me at all.' Deliberately, she shut out of her mind the memory of that rough kiss, her own heart-kicking response. 'He thinks I'm bigoted, argumentative and infuriating. And I think much the same about him,' she added, and realised too late that it might have been a good idea to let Kurt think that she was in love with Marc.

Well, that's good news anyway,' said Kurt, smiling. 'For if I thought for one second that you were attracted to such an ill-mannered boor, I would be very unhappy indeed. And I had feared. . .but no matter, now that you tell me it isn't true.'

He turned his face against hers and kissed the corner of her mouth. Then, still very gently, he pressed her back into her chair and positioned himself carefully to kiss her full on the lips. It was a long kiss, a lingering, expert kiss; it neither held back nor went too far; it ended at precisely the right moment. And it did nothing at all for her. She could only think of Marc's hard, demanding lips, of the strength in his arms, the power in his body. She moved uneasily, knowing that she must stop Kurt now, before he went any further. But to her surprise, he drew away.

'Don't be afraid, *liebling*,' he said in a whisper. 'I will not worry you any further, my Jan. As I promised, you will have time. . . But not too much, my darling, for I am human and I cannot wait indefinitely.' He gave a glance around the room, filled with moonlight, at the big bed, at the mountains that rose serenely outside. 'Marc Tyrell would no doubt think me crazy not to take advantage of this setting. So romantic—so seductive. But that is not my way, Jan. I want you to be ready

when we first come together. I want you to be as
compelled as I am. And it is my hope—my dearest
hope——' He ran a finger down her cheek and into the
hollow of her neck '—it is my hope that you will be
ready when we are at the *Schloss*—in my family home.'

He lifted himself away from her and raised her hand
to his lips, holding it there, his kiss warm in her palm,
before dropping it back lightly into her lap. And then he
was gone, moving like a cat across the room, letting
himself silently out of the door, leaving her alone.

Jan sat quite still. She looked at the mountains as if
asking them a question. As if they could tell her why
Kurt's gentleness, his professed love, the tender restraint
of his kiss, had not roused her body to any response at
all. Whereas Marc's rough kiss, his heedless passion, his
demanding hands and lips, had sent her blood
soaring. . .

But the mountains gazed back impassively. And she
knew they had no answer.

CHAPTER SIX

'So this is where it all happened. This is where Holmes and Moriarty fought together, and went over the brink of the Falls.'

Jan stepped nearer to the low wall which ran along the road at the top of the Reichenbach Falls, and peered over. Beneath her, the water roared in a thundering, ceaseless cascade down the rocky chasm to the valley floor, a hundred metres below. She thought of the two men, struggling together at this very spot, their feet slipping in the mud on the banks of the stream—there would have been no wall then—clinging to each other in a desperate effort to kill and survive. And then the final overbalancing, the knowledge that nothing could save them; the frantic scrabbling at rocks too slippery to grasp, at bushes too frail to sustain their own tenuous grip on the hillside. And the last horrific fall, down, down, down, through the beautiful, merciless spray. . .

'Conan Doyle must have really believed he'd done for poor old Sherlock when he wrote that,' she observed. 'He certainly meant to finish him off! And his readers must have been desperate to get him back, to be willing to believe anyone could have survived a fall down there.'

'Just shows how far the suspension of disbelief can be taken. If you want a person badly enough, you'll believe anything,' said Marc, and there was a curious note in his voice which made Jan glance up at him sharply.

'Just what's that supposed to mean?'

He met her look with a blandness that made her want to shake him.

'Why, nothing. Or everything. Anything you like,' he said, and she turned away, exasperated.

Since leaving Mürren that morning, she and Marc had maintained a frigid politeness. They had not met at breakfast—Jan had asked for hers to be sent up to her room, and when she came down discovered that Marc had had his early anyway, and gone out for a final walk. Irritated, she had gone back upstairs to finish her packing, only to be interrupted by a phone call to tell her that he was ready and waiting, hoping to catch the early train down to Lauterbrunnen. When, slightly flustered, she had hurried downstairs with her luggage, he had been in the lounge, drinking coffee and chatting easily with one of the young waitresses, looking as relaxed as if he'd had all the time in the world.

Neither Kurt nor Renate had been anywhere to be seen, and Jan was thankful for the chance of a breathing space, to gather her thoughts. Not that Marc seemed inclined to give her much time for thinking. His mind this morning was clearly focused entirely upon the job in hand, and he had evidently decided to use the journey time for a working discussion. Jan's brain was kept busy the whole way, from the short train ride down to Lauterbrunnen and then throughout the car journey to Meiringen, answering questions and working out ideas for the rest of the series.

'Wimsey, we'll have to include him,' Marc decided. 'There's that bell-ringing book, *The Nine Tailors*, that could have some good sequences. Great metal mouths swinging over the terrified victim. . . And what about a bit of horse-racing—Dick Francis? Of course, he doesn't actually use one detective. His heroes get mixed up in crime accidentally. We'll have to give a bit of thought to that. What other ideas have you had?'

Jan shook her head. 'I've been concentrating on the two we came here to research: Bond and Holmes. There's a lot more material in those two—they went to so many places.'

'And you think we should too. A few more exotic holidays, is that your idea? The Bahamas, Bermuda. . .didn't Bond go there? I imagine the local talent is even more attractive than in Switzerland.'

Jan flushed deeply at the insinuation, but before she could reply she realised that they had arrived in Meiringen. They drove slowly through the small town and Marc stopped the car in the large car park at the foot of the funicular.

'Here we are. And this is the plaque to Sherlock Holmes himself. They take it all very seriously here, don't they—did you notice the references in the town? The Sherlock Holmes pub? We'd better call in there later on and see what it's like.'

They boarded the strange-looking funicular with its odd pantomime-style carriages, and began the journey up the cliff beside the Falls. Now and again they caught glimpses of the tumbling waters. About halfway up, the train stopped and they got out to stare at the mass of water that flung itself over the top of the cliff above; then they followed the path up to the road and peered over the low wall.

In all that time, Jan reflected, Marc had never given so much as a hint that there had ever been anything between them other than polite formality. Never once had he indicated that he even remembered those moments last night, when they had lain together in the big armchair, their bodies pressed close, urgently seeking a satisfaction that was only to be denied; when they had kissed with a desperation that now brought a flush of embarrassment to Jan's cheeks, when Marc had held and fondled her naked breasts and she had moaned with helpless pleasure. . .

The memory brought a sharp tingling to her stomach. Abruptly, she switched her thoughts to Kurt, to his romantic declaration of love. And felt nothing.

Why? *Why*? Why should Marc Tyrell, a man she despised, a man who had insulted her parents, have the power to move her? While Kurt, who had been attentive and sensitive, who had whispered romantic words in her ear and treated her with a delicacy that she had never dreamed possible in a man, failed to arouse her?

It must have been because he had come so soon after Marc. Her body had been shocked by what had gone before, shocked into a temporary frigidity. She had not been able to respond because of her shame at the way she had already responded to Marc.

And if Kurt had forgotten his reserve, his tenderness—if he too had been rough and urgent, his kiss demanding, his body hard and thrusting—would she then have felt that leaping of the blood and senses that she had felt with Marc?

She just didn't know. And, deliberately, she allowed her mind to fantasise on such a scene. No drawing back—no panic-stricken orders to Kurt to leave her room. The next step following as inevitably as night follows day; the slow movement towards the bed, the wild abandonment, the soaring peaks of an ecstasy that matched the soaring peaks outside. . .

But the face that hovered over her in this fantasy had darkened; it was no longer fair, and the hair that fell over the broad forehead was dark, as black as the night,

and the eyes were as grey as storm-clouds that fled before
a scouring wind. . .

'Penny for them?' Marc asked conversationally, and
Jan jumped and gasped. 'Or perhaps they wouldn't bear
repeating.'

For a moment or two she looked at him quite blankly.
She had been so lost in her fantasy, there above the
thundering Falls, that she had forgotten where she was
and with whom. And then she felt her face flood with
scarlet. As humiliated as if he had indeed been able to
read her mind, she turned quickly away and stared again
at the tumbling water.

'I—I was just thinking about the filming. The
Sherlock Holmes Society—they re-enact it, we ought to
use that.' She was babbling, she knew, repeating things
that had been said before. But Marc's eyes were on her,
peculiarly penetrating. 'We ought to have contacted
them before, only it was all such a rush—I'll do it as
soon as we get back. And there must be other places
around here that we can use—places that appeared in
the story. Perhaps Kurt could tell us——' She stopped,
biting her lip, her eyes dropping before Marc's ironic
gaze.

'I'm sure he will,' Marc said smoothly. 'In fact, I
imagine that Kurt could do almost anything, if he put
his mind to it. Don't you?'

They turned away and began to walk back down the
hill, taking the path that wound down through the
woods. It was very quiet; nobody else had visited the
Falls that morning.

Jan listened to his words and felt her anger rise. She
knew she should control her temper. Releasing it only
gave her away more completely than ever. But letting it
go would be such a relief—a distraction from that fantasy

which she still felt, superstitiously, that Marc could read if she let it linger in her mind. And how did he manage to creep into that, anyway? It was *Kurt* she'd been thinking about!

'I don't know what you think you mean by that!' she said hotly. 'That's if you mean anything at all—I'm beginning to wonder if anything you say has any meaning. Apart from expressing your own childish jealousy, that is.'

'Jealousy?' he asked in an amused tone. 'And why ever should I be jealous?' He ducked his head under a trailing branch.

'Why? Plenty of reasons! Because Kurt happens to be more successful than you are, for one thing. Because he's an extremely attractive man and doesn't have to work hard to get women into his bed——' She stopped abruptly, and wasn't in the least surprised when Marc took her up at once. Oh, why did she *always* have to say the wrong thing?

'So he doesn't have to work at getting women into his bed?' he said without expression. 'I take it you're speaking from personal knowledge there?'

'No, I'm not. I just know—a woman *does* know these things,' she said desperately, not sure whether Marc's tightened lips denoted either furious anger or an inclination to laugh. 'Look, just take it from me, he's attractive. And very pleasant company.' And nothing more than that, she added mentally, and knew that nothing would have induced her to admit that to Marc.

'I'll do that.' Marc sounded almost abstracted, and Jan gave him a quick glance. 'So he knows how to treat women. And I don't. That, of course, is why you've accused me once or twice of womanising. And why you responded to me last night like a house on fire.'

She stopped dead on the narrow path. Her face was burning, as if she were indeed on fire, and her heart threatened to kick its way out of her ribs. Her body felt rigid.

'That's a filthy thing to say, and exactly like you,' she said, and her voice was dry and cracked with fury. 'What happened last night——'

'Shook you to the core,' he broke in. 'Because you've been so busy persuading yourself that you hate me, you've blinded yourself to the truth.'

'And that is?'

'Oh, come on, Jan, you're a grown woman—you know what's been happening between us, ever since that first day in my office at 90s-TV. We struck sparks straight away—don't pretend we didn't. But you've been so damned keen to see that you don't get overlooked in your career that you've forgotten what it's like to be a woman. Well, last night I forced you to face up to what it meant—and you liked it. And that's what's bugging you now—because you liked it with *me*. And you didn't want to, did you? You wanted to like it with Kurt.'

The colour was so high in Jan's cheeks that it was actually painful. She stared at Marc, and to her shame felt the hot sting of tears in her eyes. Oh, no—she wasn't going to *cry*, not on top of everything else! That would be just too much. Angrily, she went to push past him, but Marc caught her arm and dragged her against him.

'Oh, no, you don't!' he growled, and lifted one hand to force her head back. She stared up into his face and felt her body quiver as she met the grey eyes. And then he was bending to her, and she closed her eyes, helpless in his iron grasp, and felt his lips touch hers.

'This is what it's like to be a woman,' he muttered, and she felt his teeth against the softness of her mouth, his tongue like an intruder, forcing its exploration. Expertly, he shaped the kiss and broke it. 'And you like it—don't you—*don't you?*'

'Marc—please——'

'That's right. Say it—say it again—*Marc, please*—I'll have you begging me before we've done, begging me to love you. I'll teach you what it is to feel, to love, and know despair. I'll teach you what you and your precious Swiss have been doing to me this past week!' He moved his lips over her face, down the slender column of her neck, into the open neck of her blouse. 'How do you think I felt when you threw me out of your room last night and I knew damned well that man would be allowed in not half an hour later? I saw him go up. . . And he saw me. He grinned at me, and I could have killed him—and you too.'

'Marc, stop it! *Stop!*' Frantically, she struggled and at last felt his grip slacken. Twisting away from him, she scrabbled back behind a tree, keeping the trunk between them as a defence. 'Have you gone mad?' she said in a trembling voice. 'I don't belong to you! What I do is none of your business. And if you touch me again, I warn you, I'll—I'll——'

'Shout for Kurt.' Marc was breathing heavily, but seemed to have recovered himself. 'All right, I get the message. OK, Jan, you win. I've never been one to push in where I'm not wanted—and, contrary to your opinion, *I* don't have to work hard for my women either. . . But it's hands off now. And I'll respect that. But it works both ways, Jan. Don't come running to me when your romantic little idyll with Kurt comes to a sticky end, that's all. As it will, my dear, as it surely will.' He rubbed a hand over his face, looking suddenly tired. 'You know something? I think you deserve each other, you two. . . And now, let's get down into the town and find some lunch. Fighting always makes one hungry, don't you find?'

Without a word, Jan turned away and set off down the twisting path through the woods. Trust Marc Tyrell to find his composure again after such a scene, while she was still panting and quivering with the emotions he had woken in her. Trust him to be able to act as if nothing had happened.

Love, indeed—and despair! He didn't know the meaning of the words. It was all talk with him. Empty talk.

Whereas she did know what they meant. What she didn't know was why she felt such despair now. So cold and empty. As if she had just lost something precious.

Something that could never be replaced.

'And this is the room where I was born.' Kurt flung open a wide oaken door that Jan guessed must have been the original, put in when the *Schloss* was built. 'My parents' room, of course, when they were alive—but I sleep here myself now.'

Jan moved slowly into the room. It was large and spacious, with panelled walls of the same weathered oak as the door. The uneven floors were covered by thick Turkish rugs, and another, exquisitely woven, hung on the wall opposite the huge four-poster bed. The deep, glowing crimson of the curtains echoed the rich, warm colours of the rugs, and although it was so large there was no sensation of chilliness in the room. Jan looked around, seeing the portraits on the walls, the old oils of landscapes, many depicting the Reichenbach Falls or other local features, and she thought of the many generations of Kurt's family who had used this room. The scenes that had taken place here, the loving and the quarrelling, the births and the deaths. And now it was Kurt's, the last to be born here.

He was standing by the window now, watching her, and as she met his eyes she knew that he was aware of what she was thinking.

'Yes, it has seen much, this room,' he said softly. 'Every heir has been born here for the past two hundred years. And now it is waiting for the next birth. Well——' he shrugged and laughed '——that is in the lap of the gods, of course. Perhaps now that the house has lost its original function and become no more than a hotel it will turn its back on the family.'

'No! How can you say that?' Impulsively, Jan turned towards him. 'You speak as if you'd done wrong in turning the castle into a hotel. As if you'll be punished. Surely you don't believe that?'

'No?' Again he shrugged. 'Perhaps—perhaps not. How can we know what fate holds in store for us, Jan? The family was dwindling already. And our riches have dwindled also—that's why I have been compelled to become a hotelier.'

She stared at him doubtfully, unwilling to find herself involved in a discussion about his family fortunes. In spite of what had happened last night, she was afraid to let herself believe that she might hold more than a superficial attraction for Kurt. 'But you enjoy your work,' she said, feeling her way. 'Your hotel in Mürren is so good. And the *Schloss* is splendid—people must love coming to stay here.' She paused and added, 'And you're the perfect host. You make everyone so welcome.'

'But of course. If one does a job, one does it well. I am sure your friend Marc Tyrell would agree with that.' Kurt raised one eyebrow and asked, 'Where is he now, by the way? I thought he might be interested to see the *Schloss* as well.'

'There were some notes he needed to make quickly—before they went out of his mind. And a couple of phone calls.' Jan had been only too thankful that Marc had declined to accompany them on their tour. Since their walk down from the Falls, the two of them had barely spoken. She had been relieved to arrive at the *Schloss* after a tense drive up the steep, winding road from the town, and to see Kurt already there, awaiting them. He must have left Mürren very shortly after they had done so this morning, and arrived in time to order the finishing touches to their rooms.

Jan wandered again around the room, her fingers stroking the silky panelling. 'It must mean a great deal to you,' she said softly, and felt Kurt come close to her, standing just at her shoulder.

'It means everything,' he said in the same quiet tone. 'Or at least, I thought it did. . .until I met you.'

There was a moment of silence. Slowly, Jan turned her head and found Kurt's face only inches away from hers, his blue eyes dark and intent.

'Kurt. . .I. . .' But what she would have said, she had no idea. At that moment steps sounded just outside the open door. The light from the passage was blocked by two figures and, for the first time since she had known him, Jan was almost thankful to see Marc Tryell looming over her, with Renate close behind.

Kurt stepped away. When he spoke, his voice was entirely under control, as pleasant and well modulated as ever.

'Ah, Marc—and Renate too. So you've found each other. We were hoping you would find time to join us, weren't we, Jan? I'm sure Marc will find much to interest him in the *Schloss*. And your room, Marc, are you satisfied with it? It is comfortable?'

'Perfectly, thank you.' Marc's eyes were on Jan. 'Sorry if we've interrupted anything.'

'Of course you haven't! What is there to interrupt?' said Jan, and knew from Marc's sardonic glance that she had spoken too quickly. 'Kurt was just telling me the history of this room,' she added lamely. 'He was born here.'

'Indeed, that's quite true.' Renate moved forward and stood in a shaft of sunlight, her hair shimmering with the gold of afternoon. She was wearing a full skirt of fine dark blue cotton that swung like a bell when she moved, and her full breasts were outlined by a thin, clinging white sweater. 'All the children of Kurt's family are born in this room.' She turned and smiled up at Marc's dark face. 'A fine tradition, *nicht wahr?*'

'Fascinating.' But although his tone was ironic, Marc did look around the room with considerable interest. 'It's a fine room, Brunner—I can well see why you want to keep it for yourself. I imagine it is never let?'

'Never.' The Swiss's voice was clipped, as if he suspected Marc of wanting to move into the room himself. 'It is kept always for me, when I am here. One day it will be the room I share with my wife—the mother of my children.'

'And they'll be born in that bed—just as you were,' Renate said huskily, and swept back her hair with one slender hand. She turned her head to Jan, and her smile gleamed. 'Imagine it, Jan—lying here with a newborn son in your arms, knowing that everything you can see around you will one day be his!'

'Yes, Jan,' Marc said drily, 'just imagine it.'

Jan felt her face burn. She knew Kurt's eyes were on

her, but she couldn't look up and meet them—not with Marc there. Restlessly, she moved around the room, looking at the pictures and asking questions in a high, unnatural voice. Once she turned and caught Marc's gaze on her. Damn the man! Why did he always seem able to read her mind? She was sure that he knew perfectly well how confused she was—and why. Probably better than she did herself, she reflected bitterly.

'And so these are your parents.' She looked up at the family group. The father was like Kurt—tall, blond, commanding. He stood upright, almost rigid, his hand resting on the shoulder of the woman seated in front of him. Jan examined her face with interest—sweet, with a hint of resignation in the small features.

'They must have died quite young,' she said thoughtfully. 'Surely they wouldn't be so very old now?'

'In their seventies.' Kurt came to stand beside her. 'My mother died when I was only ten—she was never strong, you understand. And my father was killed twelve years ago, in a sailing accident on the Brienzee. A sudden storm. . .these things happen. It was after that that I decided the *Schloss* must work for its living. His death brought financial problems, you see—or should I say, they came to light then.'

'I see.' Kurt must have been about twenty-five when that happened. She wondered what his life had been like, alone with his father from the age of ten. How much influence had that proud-looking man had on his motherless son?

'Life hasn't been easy for you,' she said, still conscious of Marc at her shoulder. 'Some men might have simply sold up and lived on the proceeds. But you've made something really good out of it all.'

'You certainly have,' Marc agreed. 'A very good thing

indeed. But the Swiss are good at that, aren't they—turning disaster into triumph? Especially financially.'

Jan felt another spasm of anger. His tone, his words, had invested her remark with a meaning very different from the one she had intended. Why did he have to do it? Did it give him so much pleasure to needle her like this, through Kurt? And the fact that Kurt seemed quite oblivious to any double meanings in Marc's words somehow made it worse.

'He has worked very hard,' Renate said softly. 'He deserves his success. As does any man who can take charge of his life.' She turned to Marc, and to Jan there seemed to be some extra meaning to her words. Some message she was trying to convey to the tall Englishman.

Clearly, Renate admired Marc as much as he admired her. And, watching them, Jan felt a pang—a pang she immediately dismissed. Why should she care? Let Renate have him, if she wanted him—at least it might put an end to that infuriating chemistry that flowed between him and Jan.

'I agree,' she said, turning deliberately back to Kurt. 'You do deserve your success.'

He shrugged. 'I hope so. I've enjoyed it, as a matter of fact. Perhaps I was destined to serve, after so many generations of being served. And I find I rather like making money—even though my financial problems were solved quite quickly, I don't want to stop. There is only one thing I desire now. . .' His eyes were on the portrait again, and Jan gave him a quick glance and decided that there was no need to ask what his desire was. She only wondered why he had not already set out to achieve that desire, with the same determination as he had shown in restoring the family fortunes. Perhaps there had simply never been time; perhaps he had never met the right woman.

And then she remembered his words last night. The little scene that Marc had interrupted only half an hour ago.

But they had known each other so short a time. It wasn't possible. . .

Jan looked slowly around, and her eyes came at last to Marc Tyrell. He was standing half in the shadows. She could not tell if his gaze was directed now at her or at Renate.

But on his face was an expression so strange that she felt her heart turn over.

CHAPTER SEVEN

THE dining-room of the *Schloss* was half-full when Jan went down for dinner that evening. She stood for a moment at the door, hesitating, wondering which of the tables in the big room was hers, then smiled with relief as the head waiter came up to her.

'Miss Cartwright?' His English, like Kurt's, was impeccable. 'Your table is over here, by the window. Herr Tyrell is here already.'

Jan hadn't noticed Marc, sitting half concealed by a large potted plant. She gave him a brief nod and slipped into the chair held out for her by the waiter. Then she took up her menu.

'The trout is very good tonight,' the waiter told her, and she nodded. 'Served with our own fresh vegetables, of course. And you have placed your order already, Herr Tyrell?'

'Yes, I'm having the trout too.' Marc waited until the man had gone and then leaned across the table. 'All right, Jan, you needn't pretend to be reading the wine list—I've ordered a bottle already. And I don't intend to drink it alone, nor with a woman who insists on sulking throughout the entire meal, so you can take that look off your face.'

'I am *not* sulking——' Jan began indignantly, then caught his ironic eye. 'And *you* needn't look like *that* either!'

Marc grinned. '*Touché!*' He reached across and touched her hand. 'Look, Jan, let's call a truce, OK?

We're here to work together, and we can't do that efficiently if we keep getting across each other. So let's start again, hm?'

Jan stared at his hand, lying so close to her fingers. Suddenly, almost unbearably, she wanted to turn her own hand over, clasp his, palm to palm. She bit her lip, feeling her heart kick a little. Why did he have the power to affect her so much? She didn't even like the man! And she resented the electricity that crackled between them.

All the same, what he said made sense. They were supposed to be working together, and this apparently mutual antagonism had to be overcome if they were to make a success of the job. She thought of Lucia, among her piled-up ashtrays. Lucia, who looked like the office cleaner and had one of the most brilliant minds in TV. Lucia, who had done so much for Jan's own career. If nothing else, she owed it to the older woman to make a success of this.

With an effort, she moved her hand away from Marc's and gave him a stiff smile.

'All right, I'll go along with that. On one condition.' She kept her eyes on his. 'That you keep your distance in future. Don't touch me again. I don't want any repetition of—of last night, or this morning.'

He gave her an enigmatic glance, then lifted one shoulder. 'If you think I can restrain myself—it's not easy, you know, being exposed to your kind of magnetism, day in, day out.' He grinned at her indignant expression and raised a hand as if to ward off a blow. 'All right, all right—it was a joke. Remember jokes? Oh, come on, Jan, relax—you'll enjoy life so much more if you do, you know.'

'Perhaps,' she said coldly. 'As it happens, I can relax as well as the next person—in the right company.'

The laughter faded from his eyes and she was reminded suddenly of the evening when they had sat together watching the alpenglow over the Jungfrau, quiet and in total accord. 'Yes,' he said slowly, and she knew he was thinking of it too, 'I believe you can.'

There was a moment's silence. Then Marc said briskly, 'So. . .it's a strictly professional relationship from now on, yes? Well, you know now what you'll be missing.'

Jan sighed. 'Do you expect to have an affair with every woman you work with, Marc?'

'Not every one, no.' He grinned. 'I do pick and choose, you know!'

'And I suppose I'm expected to feel flattered by that? You really do have a very high opinion of yourself.'

'If I don't, no one else will.' Their starters arrived and Marc gave the pretty young waitress a smile that left her looking quite devastated. 'Didn't you know, Jan, that people take you at your own valuation? Go about apologising for your existence and they begin to think there's good reason for an apology. Tell them you're something special and they believe you. Which would you prefer?'

'I prefer to be accepted for what I am.'

'Oh, lord, we still are on our high horse!' He grimaced mockingly and began on his melon cocktail. 'And no doubt you'll add to that the inevitable rider *as a woman*.'

'As a *person*,' Jan corrected him, and he raised his eyes to the ceiling.

'As a person, then. Jan, does it never occur to you that you *are* accepted as a person? That everyone I know admires you for the work you do in exactly the same way as they would if you were a man? You're preaching to the converted, Jan—there's no sexism in our job. We're all in there pitching together. And if we get the odd twinge of pleasure from looking at a pretty face or figure, or adding a little spice of romance to the daily grind, what's so wrong with that? I'm all for it!'

'You would be,' she retorted automatically, but his words struck home. It was true that she'd never been exposed to any discrimination because of her sex. 'But that's all because of people like my mother,' she insisted. 'She and others like her have worked hard to achieve what we have today. And we're not going to let it go now. Why should we?'

'Why, indeed? But you seem to think that if you relax for one moment we wicked men are going to wrest your advantages away from you and have you back in the mines, dragging coal. Or back at the kitchen sink. A woman's place, in the home—and the home a cage. That's what you're afraid of, isn't it?' He shook his head. 'Jan, I'm sorry for you. You've lost sight of real life, you and your mother and others like you. You see peeling potatoes as a humiliation, looking after your own children as a chore. And you're wrong—sadly wrong. We all have to survive, and to survive we have to do the potato-peeling. And as for bringing up kids—that's the future, Jan. Haven't you ever heard that the hand that rocks the cradle rules the world?'

'Of course I've heard that,' Jan said shortly.

'But you don't believe it. You think it's just another example of masculine propaganda designed to keep the little woman happy.' Marc thrust his plate away. 'All right, we won't discuss it any more. I can see we'll never agree on this—even though basically I'm on your side. But you don't want to accept that, do you? You don't want to see men as reasonable creatures—the whole idea's been brainwashed out of you.'

'That's rubbish! There are men and men, and some of

them I get along with very well indeed. My father, for
one——'

'Your father's been carefully trained,' Marc said
abruptly. 'It's nothing short of cruelty, what's been done
to him.'

'—and Kurt Brunner,' Jan finished, her anger rising
at Marc's interruption. 'Now Kurt is a *really* understanding man.' She gave him a swift glance of triumph. That
would deflate his overblown ego!

But Marc didn't react. He said nothing while the
waitress removed their empty plates. Then, as they
waited for the main course, he remarked as if they'd
done nothing but exchange pleasantries for the last
twenty minutes, 'I thought the Falls were quite dramatic,
didn't you?'

Jan blinked, but decided to follow his lead. Their
truce hadn't exactly started well, after all. Perhaps they
should try again.

'Yes,' she said, 'I did. They'll make good filming. And
the *Schloss*,' she went on smoothly. 'It really is quite
something. We ought to be able to use it in some way.
Kurt's bedroom, for instance—a dreadful waste not to
do something in there, wouldn't you say?'

Marc gave her a sharp glance and she hid a smile,
keeping her expression completely bland and her eyes
grave. For once, she felt that he did not know what she
might be thinking.

'All that history,' she continued. 'Conan Doyle may
even have met the family—what would it have been,
Kurt's grandfather, great-grandfather? Maybe we could
turn something up—we could use Kurt himself in an
interview.'

'I don't think so,' Marc said abruptly. 'That would be
quite against the spirit of the series.'

'Oh, do you think so?' Jan asked innocently. 'But we're planning to do similar things in some of the other programmes. The Wimsey one you were talking about— we'll be using present-day bellringers. What's the difference? And if Kurt's family actually did meet Conan Doyle——'

'We've no evidence that they did.' His voice was terse. 'Let's leave Brunner out of this, Jan, all right?' He glanced restlessly about the big dining-room. 'I'm beginning to wish we hadn't agreed to come here. The other hotel would have been perfectly adequate. And the whole set-up's obviously proving too much of a distraction for you.'

'My relationship with Kurt is none of your business——' Jan began hotly, but he broke in on her words.

'I didn't mention your relationship, as you call it. I said the set-up——'

'It's what you meant, all the same. And it seems to me it's more of a distraction for you than for me.' She glared at him across the table. 'You can't forget it, can you? You can't accept that another man might be more attractive than you are? You want to be top dog all the time—leader of the pack—the stag with his own harem, fighting off all other comers. And the fact that one woman can resist you and prefers another man has really got your goat.'

'You make me sound like a zoo!' he jeered. 'Better get your metaphors sorted out, Jan. . . And as it happens, you're quite wrong about me. I'm not out for conquests. And what annoys me about you isn't the fact that you *can* resist me, but that you *can't*. You're trying to convince yourself, all the time, that it's this Kurt who keeps you lying awake at night—oh yes, I've seen the dark circles under your eyes—that it's Kurt who makes your heart jump when he looks at you, when he touches you. And it's not. He means nothing to you, Jan. But you won't admit it, even to yourself. You're not only self-deluding, you're downright dishonest. And it's going to lead you into trouble.' He stopped, then went on, 'Well, don't come running to me when it all blows up in your face. I wash my hands of you.'

Jan stared at him. Her face, burning when he first began to speak, had lost all its colour. She could feel the blood receding, leaving her sick and faint. She shook her head, feeling anger and distress war within her, then she rose shakily to her feet.

'You can eat my trout,' she said in a trembling voice. 'I'm not hungry any more.'

And she turned and almost fled from the room.

So much for their truce.

Much later, as she sat at the window in her room watching the moon rise over the mountains, she heard a knock on the door.

For a moment, she didn't move. It could be either Marc or Kurt, but she didn't feel inclined to go and find out. If it was Marc, she certainly didn't want to see him. And if it was Kurt—she felt too confused to know what her reaction might be.

The knock came again, and she knew she would have to answer. Reluctantly she got to her feet and went slowly across the room, switching on the light as she went. Moonlight was altogether too evocative, especially when it was lighting the mountains with that unearthly glow. And Jan didn't feel she could cope with any more emotion that night.

But it was neither Marc nor Kurt who stood at her

door. Instead, to her surprise, she found the pretty young waitress who had served them at dinner.

'Mr Tyrell said you were feeling tired and had decided to have some supper upstairs,' she said, and Jan saw that she was holding a tray. 'He asked to have this sent up to you.'

'Oh—thank you. Come in.' Startled, Jan stood back and the girl entered the room and set the tray down on a low table. It contained a plate with some salad and cold meat, a bowl of fruit, a small cheese platter and a carafe of wine. The girl arranged the food neatly and smiled at Jan.

'There. Is good?'

'It looks very good,' Jan said. 'Thank you very much—er—I don't know your name.'

'I am called Heidi.'

'Oh, that's pretty,' said Jan. 'I read a book about a girl called Heidi when I was a child.'

The girl smiled. 'It is a common name here. Now, if you have everything you want, I must go. I shall bring some coffee later if you wish it.'

'Yes,' Jan said, 'that would be very nice.'

She waited until Heidi had gone and then looked again at the tray. So Marc had asked for this to be sent up! What did that mean—that he was feeling guilty about his behaviour? Or that he simply didn't want his researcher to starve? She sighed, then sat down and picked up the plate of salad. What did it matter, after all? She was hungry, and he'd sent her some food, and she certainly wasn't going to be so childish as to refuse it.

The salad was delicious and the wine exactly to her taste. Suddenly realising how hungry she was, she cleared the plate. She finished with fruit and cheese and then sat back, feeling better. Her feelings towards Marc had mellowed. Perhaps she had reacted a little too hastily. He had, after all, suggested a truce in the first place. And he was right in saying that there wasn't any sexism at 90s-TV—well, not much, anyway. Jan guessed that there was always going to be the odd man who considered femininity as a synonym for second-class. The man whose own ego was in jeopardy. And it was quite true that Marc hadn't actually expressed any chauvinistic sentiments, and he did listen to her ideas and frequently accept them.

All the same, nobody could be expected to sit and listen to the kind of things he'd said about her parents and not react. That had been quite unforgivable. Jan tried to push away the uncomfortable picture of her father emerging from his study with a newspaper in his hand. A crossword half done, or a detective story half read. Was that really his life? Did he ever accompany his wife anywhere now? Jan tried hard to remember, but she knew that in the past few years her parents had rarely been seen together in public, except for those occasions when it had suited Susan Cartwright to have a husband in tow. In tow. . .that phrase described their relationship exactly.

And as for her mother—it was easier to recall that energetic, bustling figure, always busy with an article, a book or a TV appearance. Susan Cartwright was a personality impossible to ignore. The fact that she'd been easy to dislike had never worried her—popularity had been something she'd never sought as she'd aired her opinions. Influence had been enough, and she'd enjoyed plenty of that.

And Marc's right, Jan thought. She's influenced me. And what's wrong with that? She's right—isn't she?

But she knew that in the past few months—since she'd started working at 90s-TV—she had begun to wonder about that. After all, could anyone ever be *completely* right?

For the next few days, Marc worked Jan like a slave-driver. Coolly detached, totally unemotional, he behaved as if they had never shared any moments other than those that were completely relevant to their work. Even her reluctant effort to thank him for sending supper to her room was met with no more than a brusque nod of the head, and she retired into herself, baffled and vaguely hurt.

But she was given no time to nurse her feelings. Every minute was taken up with the programme and its planning. Together they tramped round Meiringen, looking for shots that would look good on screen. They went into the Sherlock Holmes pub, travelled again on the funicular to the top of the Falls, clambered down through the woods, assessing the best views. Marc talked endlessly into the small pocket tape recorder he carried everywhere, and Jan made copious notes of her own. In the evenings, after dinner, she retired to her room to type them up on her portable typewriter while Marc ran through the videos he had shot during the day as 'roughs' for the cameraman to see. By the time they had gone over the work done that day and decided on tomorrow's plan, Jan was too exhausted to do anything more than fall into bed and go straight to sleep.

'When will he give you some time off, this man who works you so hard?' Kurt asked plaintively as she sat at breakfast, reading over her notes from the day before. 'I thought that while you were here, we might have a little time together. But since that first day, I've hardly seen you.'

'Well, we don't have all that much time,' said Jan, brushing back her curls as she shook the papers into order. 'We've got to be back in London next week, there are other programmes to plan as well, and I've still got some work to do on the last programme I did—the editing's finished now and the director wants me to see the run-through. And then there's——'

'No!' Kurt caught at her wrists and held them firmly. 'I don't wish to hear! It seems to me that you work much too hard, Jan. Women shouldn't have to give up all their time in this way. Where is your life going? Where is the pleasure of simply being—a woman? The pretty dresses, the parties. . .the romance?' Keeping his eyes on hers, he lifted her hands to his lips. 'I had hoped we might get to know each other a little better,' he said softly.

Jan looked at him and felt a guilty blush creep into her cheeks. If she were honest, she knew she would have to admit that she had welcomed the hard work and long hours, looking on them as an excuse for keeping out of Kurt's way. She had been feeling distinctly uncomfortable about him ever since that first afternoon, when he had shown her his bedroom and talked of his children being born there, of finding the right woman to share his life. She still found it difficult to believe that he really saw her as the right woman. . .but, just in case he did, she was determined not to let the subject arise again. Nor did she want any repetition of the night at Mürren, when he had kissed her and talked of the joy they would share together at the *Schloss*. It wasn't fair to let anything like that happen again—much better to keep him at arm's length.

But even that wasn't really fair, she acknowledged

miserably. Kurt had been so generous. Wasn't it rather churlish to pretend to be busier than she was, just to avoid him? Couldn't she offer him her friendship, even if she could give him nothing else?

'Kurt, I'm sorry,' she said impulsively. 'I've been neglecting you. And I was hoping we'd have some time together too.' Careful. Don't overdo it! 'Look, Marc doesn't need me this afternoon—why don't you show me round the grounds of the *Schloss*? I've still not seen them all. That's if *you've* got time,' she added with a smile. 'After all, you're busy too.'

'Never too busy for you, my dear Jan,' he declared. 'And yes, I shall certainly keep this afternoon free for you. But I have a better idea. We shall go right away from here—perhaps out on the lake, where nobody can come and say you must work or ask me where the clean sheets are kept.' Jan laughed aloud at the idea of Kurt's impeccably trained staff ever asking him such a question. 'I have a motor yacht there and we could be quite alone.' He looked at her, his eyes suddenly grave. 'It will be a good thing for us to do,' he said quietly.

She stared back at him, her heart thumping suddenly. Would it really be a good thing? She wasn't so sure. An afternoon alone on a motor yacht, out in the middle of the Brienzee—she could foresee all kinds of problems arising.

But Kurt wasn't like Marc, ready to take any opportunity that came his way. He was a gentleman—and if his old-fashioned courtesy had got on her nerves, it might also prove a protection. Surely she would be safe?

As she hesitated, her eye caught a movement at the end of the dining-room. She shifted her gaze slightly and saw Marc standing at the door. He was with Renate and they were laughing at each other. There was an intimacy in the way that they were standing, close enough for their arms to touch, in the way that their eyes were meeting, that stabbed at her heart.

It was the first morning that Marc had not been down to breakfast before her. The first morning she'd seen him looking quite so relaxed.

As she watched them, Marc moved and looked across the room. His eyes met hers, then she saw them travel to Kurt and take in the way he was holding her hands, the look on his face. She saw his expression freeze and harden.

Deliberately, Jan returned her glance to Kurt. She smiled at him.

'I'd love to come on your yacht with you this afternoon,' she said. 'It sounds heavenly!'

The little town of Brienz was quiet as Jan and Kurt wandered slowly through its narrow streets that afternoon. The tourist season was not yet fully under way, and many of the visitors had disappeared in the direction of the Ballenburg Open-Air Museum, with its collection of buildings from all the Swiss regions. If Jan had been able to choose, she would have asked to go there, to explore the different houses and watch the demonstrations of cheese-making, weaving and basket-making that took place each day. But, impulsively, she had agreed to go to Kurt's yacht, and it was impossible to change the plan now.

'What a fascinating little town,' she remarked as they stepped carefully over the tracks of the railway that ran beside the main road. 'Oh, and look at that little steam train! It's like a toy. Where does it go?'

'To the top of the Rothorn, nearly three hundred and fifty metres above the town—see?' Kurt pointed up to the summit towering above them. 'Quite an interesting drive—something you must do next time you come.' He spoke quite casually, as if her next visit had already been discussed and arranged. 'But today we spend on the water, *ja*?'

'Oh. . .yes.' Feeling even more uncomfortable, Jan sought for ways to delay their voyage. 'But do let's look around here first. Can we look at some of these shops? They may be closed by the time we come back.' She stopped at a window filled with elaborate wood-carvings, and was reminded sharply of the little carved otter she had seen in Marc's office back at 90s-TV. She thought again of their first meeting there, the way he had stood at the window, running his fingers almost sensuously down its curving spine. And she drew away from Kurt's lightly moving fingertips.

Once again she felt that Marc had driven her into a corner. She would never have agreed to coming on this trip if she hadn't seen his face as he watched her and Kurt at the breakfast table. If she hadn't seen the way he'd looked at Renate. . .

'Brienz is the home of the Swiss wood-carving industry,' Kurt observed as they stood on the pavement. 'Almost all the shops sell something in wood—see, many of them are very intricate indeed. People buy them for souvenirs, of course.'

'Yes—nobody goes home from Switzerland without a cuckoo clock,' smiled Jan. 'And there are nearly as many different kinds of cuckoo clock as there are cuckoos! Why *are* the Swiss so cuckoo about cuckoos?'

Kurt looked at her and she grinned ruefully. Well, it hadn't been a very good joke—but she couldn't suppress the feeling that Marc would have at least deemed it worthy of a chuckle. That was one thing they did share—

a sense of humour, which had helped them through quite a lot of the irritations of their journey. Whereas Kurt didn't seem to have much sense of humour at all. Or perhaps it was just different.

'Where do you keep your yacht?' she asked, and he turned eagerly and led her down a narrow alleyway between the shops. At the end, she could see the bright, shimmering blue of the lake and the green of the mountains beyond, and in a few minutes she found herself emerging on to a small quay.

There were a good many boats here, bobbing gently on the tiny waves, their halliards tinkling against their masts. Jan looked at them with interest, wondering which was Kurt's. That large one there with its gleaming superstructure, its glass-enclosed cabin with wide sliding doors leading to the cockpit? Or that small one, slightly shabby, its decks littered with tar-encrusted ropes and an eager look about its blunt little bows, as if it couldn't wait to get back out on to the water again?

No, she didn't think Kurt's yacht would be either small or shabby. And she was not surprised when he led her, not to the glossy vessel she had first seen, but to an even larger and glossier one that was moored in what was obviously the best place on the quay, towering over the rest and looking more like a miniature version of an ocean liner than a yacht designed to spend all its time on an inland sea.

As they approached, an elderly man came out of the cabin, wiping his hands on a fistful of cotton waste, and sketched a salute. Kurt spoke to him in rapid German and he nodded and climbed on to the jetty.

'This is Franz, who looks after the *Hasli* for me,' Kurt explained. 'I've just told him he can have the afternoon off—I can manage the yacht alone, and we don't need company, do we?' He smiled at Jan, his blue eyes crinkling at the corners, and she thought again how handsome he looked, standing there with the sunshine turning his hair to gold, deepening the tan on his already bronze skin, smiling with those perfect teeth. And wondered just why it was that she simply wasn't attracted to him; why even now she could not help thinking what it would be like to be here with Marc, about to set out together on uncharted waters. . .

Her heart bumped. But it wasn't just the idea of a yacht trip. With a sudden, unexpected yearning, she knew that it was the thought of any time off at all with Marc—the thought of moments, hours, days, spent just relaxing together, whether sailing, swimming, walking or simply *being*. Getting to know each other; sharing. . .

Franz strolled off along the quay and Kurt stepped down into the cockpit of the yacht and turned to offer Jan his hand. She hesitated, then took his outstretched hand and stepped down after him. And immediately realised her mistake.

Keeping her hand in his, Kurt drew her close against him. With those sky-blue eyes that were so devastatingly attractive and which did so very little for her, he smiled down at her. And bent his head to kiss her firmly and lingeringly on the mouth.

'Let's go, Jan,' he said huskily as she stared up at him. 'Let's get away from here. I've been waiting for this for so long. . .'

CHAPTER EIGHT

THE yacht trip had turned out, after all, quite differently from what Jan had expected.

For a start, she had expected that, once they were alone, Kurt would take the opportunity of—well, of mooring somewhere quiet, perhaps, or tying up to a buoy, and then repeating the protestations of love that he'd hinted at so often during the past week. She had anticipated it with a sinking heart, aware that if Kurt refused to take no for an answer she would be in serious trouble. Not that she thought for a moment that he would try to force her—Kurt's old-world courtesy would never have allowed such a thing, she was sure—but she knew from experience that a man who was determined to persist could be very difficult indeed to handle. And an isolated yacht, with no way of escape and no one near to provide distraction, was not the place to be with such a man.

If it hadn't been for Marc, she thought again, she would never be here. But there was something about him, the way he looked at her with that scornful challenge in his eyes, the way his lips twisted when he surveyed her with Kurt, that drove her to want to do something—anything—to annoy him. And for some reason, the sight of her with Kurt *did* seem to annoy him. Just as the sight of him with Renate seemed to turn a knife in her own breast.

I won't let him affect me! she thought crossly, sitting in the cockpit as Kurt started the engine and cast off.

Why should it matter, after all? It's not as if he means anything to me. It's not as if I love him.

She didn't love him. . .did she?

Jan turned her head angrily and stared out across the lake. Forget him! she told herself forcibly. Get him out of your mind. He's got no right to be there—no right at all.

She looked at Kurt, standing tall at the wheel, his corn-gold hair lifting in the wind created by their speed. He had removed his shirt and she could see the muscles rippling under his bronzed skin. His teeth flashed as he smiled at her, and she smiled back. Why couldn't she fall in love with him? Why *couldn't* she?

But once again, as he had kissed her when she'd first got into the boat, she had felt nothing. Absolutely nothing. And it was all—she was convinced—the fault of Marc Tyrell.

Because it was Marc who set her skin on fire. Marc who made her ache deep down inside with the desire to touch him. Marc who haunted her dreams, who invaded her thoughts, making every moment, sleeping or waking, a torment.

And she didn't even *like* him—much less love him. Did she?

That was a question she didn't even want to ask. Loving Marc Tyrell, she suspected, wouldn't be easy. He was a difficult man, demanding and unrelenting in his demands. He wanted the best from everyone and saw no reason why he shouldn't have it. He wanted the best from her as a researcher—already he'd stretched her, drawing from her a depth of capability she hadn't known she had. He would demand as much of her if she were a lover—or a wife. And the thought made her shiver, even though her fear was mixed with a curious, tingling excitement and a deep longing.

But it was ridiculous to think this way! She was never going to be on those terms with Marc Tyrell. She didn't want to be—and if she did, there was no chance of it now. Not now that Renate had come along.

Feeling suddenly bleak, Jan looked out across the dancing waves, blinking her eyes against the dazzling sunlight. If only she could love Kurt instead. Wouldn't it be easier. . .more peaceful. . .more secure?

The boat sped along through the water, splintering the dancing blue with twin walls of foaming white. The sun, beating down on her face, was cooled by a steady breeze. To either side rose the mountains, green and wooded on their lower slopes, soaring to peaks of glimmering snow and ice. Here and there the slopes were rent by ragged valleys and gorges, sparkling with glittering cascades.

Kurt put out a hand and she went to sit beside him. He slipped his arm around her waist and held her against his side. She could feel the warmth of his skin through her thin shirt.

'It is beautiful, *nicht wahr*?' he said in her ear, and she felt the brush of his lips. 'You like our country, *ja*?'

'I love it,' Jan said honestly. 'I don't think there's anywhere quite like Switzerland. So clear—so clean. So ordered. And beauty everywhere you look.'

'Ah yes. We take care of our heritage. We don't neglect it as some countries do. And we love order. It's a good thing.'

'Yes.' Jan spoke a little hesitantly. 'But not *too* much, Kurt. It doesn't do to have everything too well behaved.'

He slanted a look down at her. 'No? In what way, Jan?'

She blushed, thinking of the interpretation Marc would immediately have put upon her words. 'Well, it isn't really natural to have everything perfect, is it? All straight lines and clean-cut and predictable. You need a few little imperfections here and there to make things interesting. Don't you agree?'

'No,' said Kurt, 'I don't think I do. Order is important, Jan. Everything in its own place. Everything cared for so that it performs in the best way possible. Perfection is the ideal—it must be. What is wrong with that?'

'I don't quite know,' Jan said after a pause. 'Except that if you expect people to be perfect, you're going to be disappointed. Nobody can live up to that.'

'Oh, come, Jan,' he said easily. 'I am sure *you* could.'

She turned quickly and looked at him. He was smiling. He looked confident, sure of himself—and of her. She shook her head quickly and tried to move away, but his arm held her firmly.

'No, Kurt! You mustn't think that—that I'm perfect. I'm not—nobody is. It's not fair to expect it. Human beings *aren't.*'

He laughed. 'Oh, Jan! As if I do! Of course you are not perfect. Of course you're human. Why, I could tell you of half a dozen imperfections at this very moment— but such very tiny ones. In everything important—in my eyes—you're as perfect as any woman could be. Doesn't it please you to know that?'

They had reached a small bay, surrounded by deep woods. He switched off the engine and let the boat drift gently as he turned and took her in his arms.

Here it came. This was what she had expected, waited for with such dread.

'Doesn't it please you to know how I feel?' he murmured.

She shook her head. 'No. I'm sorry, Kurt, but it doesn't. I don't want anyone to think I'm perfect, or even better than I am.'

'Not even the man you love?'

'*Especially* the man I love,' she insisted. 'Kurt, we all have clay feet—I'd want the man I loved to know mine right from the beginning and love me just the same. If I felt that he'd think less of me when he found them out— I'd be worried all the time. And I'd know our love was based on something false—don't you understand that?'

'So tell me about your clay feet,' he said comfortably. 'You wake up in a bad temper, is that it? No, I won't believe it! You talk too much? You don't talk enough? I don't believe in either of them. Perhaps you're untidy— or too houseproud. No, neither of those faults seems to be my Jan. You see—you have no clay feet!' He gave a laugh of triumph.

She sighed. 'You see? You're not taking me seriously at all.'

'Maybe that's because I don't need to,' he said, folding his arms around her. 'Maybe it's because today isn't a day for being serious, but for being happy—happy that we've found each other, happy that we're together. Let's forget about clay feet and imperfections, Jan. This is a day for perfect harmony—a day for lovers, a day to be remembered.'

He was right, Jan thought as she felt his warm strength against her soft breasts and looked at the clear sky, the dazzling water, the deep green of the trees. It was a day for lovers, a day for harmony, for memories. But only if you were with the right person.

And Kurt wasn't the right one for her. He never could be.

'Kurt,' she began as he nuzzled her neck, his lips warm against her skin. 'Kurt, please—listen to me——'

'Did I say you didn't talk too much?' he whispered. 'Don't talk now, Jan. Just let's be together and enjoy it. Let's be happy that destiny brought us to each other.'

'But it didn't!' Frantic now to stop this before it went any further, she twisted away from him. She stared into his surprised eyes. 'Kurt, you must listen to me! Whatever it is you feel for me, I—I don't feel it for you. I'm sorry, I wish I did—but I don't, and that's all there is to it.' She turned away and gripped the coaming, staring down into the water. 'I didn't mean to lead you on,' she said shakily. 'It just seemed to—happen. But I can't love you, and I can't let you think that I do.' She faced him again. 'Maybe now you'll see my clay feet,' she said tremulously.

Kurt stared at her and then, to her astonishment, his face split into a smile. He stepped forward and laid his hands on her shoulders.

'My poor Jan! My poor little English *liebling*. Don't look so upset, my sweet.' His fingers were gentle and she didn't try to twist away again. She looked up at him uncertainly. 'I've gone too quickly for you,' he said tenderly. 'I've rushed you too much. You must forgive me—that is one of *my* faults, to be too impulsive. Jan, don't look so afraid. I shan't rush you again. I am happy to wait—until you feel more certain.' His smile was as confident as before. 'I know everything will work out for us.'

Jan felt helpless. 'Kurt, you're still not listening to me. It *won't* work out—not in the way you think. I've told you, I don't feel that way about you. I never will.'

'Never is a big word, Jan.'

'It's true, all the same.'

He regarded her steadily for a few minutes. Then he said quietly, 'Is there someone else, Jan? Someone back in England?'

She shook her head. 'No. There's no one else.'

'And Marc? He isn't——?'

'Marc doesn't like me any more than I like him,' she said steadily. 'We're colleagues, nothing else.' And she wondered a little at the hollowness she felt inside her.

He kept his eyes on her a little longer. Then she felt his fingers relax. He smiled again and his teeth flashed against his suntan.

'Then there is nothing to fear,' he said comfortably. 'And as I've already told you, Jan, I am happy to wait. You are worth waiting for.'

Before she could say another word, he had started the engine again. The boat lifted its bows and surged out of the little bay. And for the rest of the afternoon, as they swept along the length of the sunlit Brienzee, he stood tall and handsome at the wheel, the confident smile never leaving his face, while Jan sat helpless at his side and wondered how she would ever make him believe her.

When she came down to dinner that evening, she found Renate already sitting at the table Jan usually shared with Marc, drinking one of Kurt's gaily coloured cocktails and laughing, apparently at something Marc had just said. She looked up as Jan arrived and gave her a wide, friendly smile.

'Jan—here you are at last! Marc has been entertaining me with stories of British television—I had no idea all that went on behind the scenes! Come and sit down and tell me if it is all really true.'

'I can't tell you that, without knowing what he's been telling you.' Jan looked at Marc, who met her gaze.

'Actually, I've been waiting in the lounge—I thought you might be wanting a discussion this evening.'

'No, I thought we'd give that a miss tonight,' he said easily. 'Take a few hours off. We've been pretty well hard at it ever since we arrived in Switzerland—won't do us any harm to give the poor tired brains a rest.'

'I see. I rather wish you'd told me that,' Jan said with a stiffness in her voice. 'I needn't have spent my time looking over the schedules and thinking of fresh angles.'

'Oh, I'm sure it won't have been a waste of time. I'll have a look at them tomorrow, some time.' He grinned at her and turned back to Renate. 'Jan's quite a little workaholic, if you understand that word.'

'Workaholic. . . Like alcoholic, you mean? Addicted to work?' Renate laughed. 'Surely not? She looks far too sensible.'

Sensible, Jan thought wryly. Is that really what I look like? No wonder I can't compete with glamour queens like Renate! And she looked down at her simple blue dress, comparing it with Renate's equally simple yet infinitely more stunning silver sheath.

Infinitely more expensive too, I'd guess, she thought. TV researchers weren't paid designer prices. All the same, she'd never been particularly dissatisfied with her appearance—until tonight. She glanced at Marc and saw that his eyes were on the blonde Swiss girl. He wouldn't have noticed if Jan had been wearing a strip of hessian tied with string.

She sat almost silent through the meal, feeling like an interloper between these two who had evidently so quickly reached an accord. And she had to admit that Renate made a charming companion. Laughing, good-humoured and with a ready wit that could also be incisively sharp, she sparred with Marc, refusing to let him get away with even a hint of sexism, yet keeping a smile on her face—and on his—all the time. And all in a voice so seductively husky that Jan wondered more than once how she had ever managed to stay single for so long—for she must, surely, be into her thirties. Perhaps she enjoyed it that way, Jan thought with a flash of malice—perhaps she liked to play the field. Perhaps she was the kind of woman who got her kicks from stealing other girls' men. . . But she was instantly ashamed of the thought. Renate had shown her nothing but friendliness—flirtatious though she might be with Marc, there was none of the catty backbiting that many attractive women indulged in when competing for a man.

And anyway, she wasn't competing, was she? Not for Marc. Hadn't he given her a chance? And when she'd refused it, hadn't he said quite plainly that he'd washed his hands of her?

It was no use having regrets now, Jan thought. And why did she have to keep reminding herself that she didn't want Marc anyway? She watched the other two with an ache in her heart. They were talking softly now, smiling with an intimacy that made her feel suddenly cold, lonely, isolated. With a moment of miserable clarity, she knew that deep inside she longed for the kind of intimacy they seemed to share. She wanted someone to love—someone who would love her. She didn't want to be alone any longer.

Kurt did not appear during the meal, but arrived, smiling, as they were beginning their coffee. He sat down beside Jan, and touched her hand briefly.

'Did you think I was neglecting you? I am sorry— there were some new guests who needed attention, and then a problem in the kitchen. . .' He raised his eyebrows comically, inviting sympathetic laughter at the lot of a hotelier. 'But I am free now for the rest of the evening, unless there is an emergency, so why don't we all go for a walk in the grounds? It's not dark yet and there'll be a moon later—it can be very beautiful out there on an evening like this.'

'Oh, yes, let's!' Renate exclaimed at once, and turned to Marc. 'You will come, won't you, Marc? The sight of the *Schloss* as the moon rises is one not to be missed.'

'Then of course we mustn't miss it,' said Marc, and smiled at her.

Jan turned away. It was sickening, the way those two carried on! She laid her hand over Kurt's, knowing that Marc would notice. 'It sounds lovely.'

Once outside, they began to walk along the woodland path leading away from the sweeping lawns that lay in front of the *Schloss*, splitting up quite naturally into two couples. Marc and Renate were ahead, and Jan watched them, her mind only half on what Kurt was saying. They made a magnificent pair, she thought. Renate was only a few inches shorter than Marc, her gleaming blonde hair a shining foil for his dark head, her voluptuous figure almost slight beside the breadth of his shoulders and back. And as the Swiss girl tilted her head a little—quite unnecessarily, Jan thought—to look at him and laugh, she felt a stab of pain that she just wasn't quick enough to hide.

It was almost as if she were jealous! But she couldn't be—not of Renate and Marc Tyrell.

'Such a beautiful evening,' Kurt said softly. 'And I am so fortunate to be walking here with the woman I have spent my life searching for.' He smiled at her and she sighed. Hadn't her words that afternoon had any effect at all? How was she going to make him see that she meant what she had said? Once again she wished she could respond to him. So many girls would have done. His words held all the romance of the novels her mother had dismissed as rubbish—and yet she felt there was something missing, a lack of something solid, real. It was almost as if he were playing a part.

'Kurt,' she said in a low voice, 'you must listen to me. We've known each other such a short time. . .and I'll be leaving in a day or two——'

'Ah, don't speak of it! It tears my heart to think of Switzerland without you.'

'But we have to speak of it.' She hesitated, wondering how to express herself. After all, Kurt had made no positive suggestions—he hadn't actually proposed. 'Kurt, you've talked about us—about our lives——'

'One life,' he interrupted, taking her hand and gazing earnestly into her eyes. 'One life only, Jan—a shared life, surely? It has a happy sound to it, don't you agree? A good sound.'

'Yes, it sounds very good.' She glanced at him again. 'But, Kurt, you can't really believe, after only a week— we hardly know each other——'

'I know all I need to know, Jan.' His eyes were a very dark blue, here in the shadowy wood. Marc and Renate had wandered on ahead and were out of sight. Jan stopped and looked up at him. She remembered again that theory about looking at a man's mouth if you wanted him to kiss you. Kurt's lips were finely chiselled, as perfectly even as the rest of him. . . Hastily she took her eyes away and sighed softly.

'Sad, my *liebling*?' he asked softly. 'Or is that a sigh of happiness? Say it is—say you have no more doubts. Ah, Jan, Jan!'

He moved closer, his arms encircling her, and Jan wondered again where the other two had gone. She would never have agreed to come here if she had known they would get separated—yet couldn't she have foreseen that? Wasn't it obvious that Marc had Renate would take the opportunity of slipping away into the dusk-filled woods for privacy? Wasn't it equally obvious that Kurt too would take his own advantage?

'Kurt,' she said desperately, 'you promised me time. Please. . .' She looked up into his face. 'Please take your arms away, Kurt,' she said quietly.

He looked down at her with reproach in his eyes. Did she have to feel guilty, just because he didn't attract her? Was it her fault? She moved restlessly, laid her hands against his chest, and heard the sounds of Marc and Renate returning along the path.

'So here you both are!' The Swiss girl's voice rang out, as clear and confident as Kurt's. Marc came into view and took in the scene with one swift glance.

'Seems we're interrupting something, Renate,' he said tersely. 'Maybe we should go another way.'

'No—please.' Jan found her voice. 'We were just going back—I'm feeling rather cold, I forgot to bring a jacket. And anyway, I want an early night tonight—I thought I'd go straight to bed.' She caught Marc's ironical glance and coloured. Kurt's arms dropped and she stepped quickly away. 'I'll see you all in the morning,' she said brightly. 'Sorry to break up the party.' And she began to walk rapidly across the lawn.

She was past caring what any of them thought of her. She just wanted to reach the haven of her room.

It struck Jan, as she watched the moon rise over the mountains and send its faltering light down into the lake, that she had spent too much time during this trip doing just this—sitting in her room, alone, watching a beautiful view that needed to be shared.

She went to the bathroom and snapped on the light, giving herself a critical look in the mirror. She showered, brushed her teeth, and smoothed in the cool moisturiser that was all she ever put on her skin. She ran a comb through her auburn curls and slipped into a nightdress of fine cotton lawn, with delicate lace at the neck.

As she came out of the bathroom and crossed the moonlit bedroom, she heard a soft knock at the door. She stopped, her heart thumping.

'Who——?'

The knock came again. Before she could move, the door opened quietly and a tall figure moved into the shadowy room.

'It's me, Jan. I had to come.'

'Kurt!' She stared at him, her mouth dry. He moved purposefully towards her and she backed away nervously, realising that the bed was directly behind her.

He reached for her hands. 'I had to come. I couldn't let matters stay as they were—so undecided. You seem so shy, so uncertain. If you go back to England, I might lose you.' He caught at her, gripping her wrists in fingers that were too strong to permit escape. 'Jan, I need you. I want you. Now.'

She tried to pull her hands away. 'Kurt, I've told you—it's not possible—I don't love you—I can't—please, Kurt, please believe me! There's no future for us, nothing!'

There was a small silence. Then he said, his voice as cool and remote as the peaks of the mountains all around them, 'Not possible?'

'No.' Searching for words, she let the silence continue for a moment, then said miserably, 'I've tried to tell you,

Kurt, you know I have. This afternoon, on the lake—this evening in the wood. You just won't listen. But you must believe me. You can't go on trying to convince yourself—trying to convince me. It won't work. And you'll only end up hurt.'

'And do you not think you are hurting me now?' His voice rose a little. 'Do you not think you are stabbing me to the heart? Jan, you say you've tried to tell me, but that's not true! Your eyes, your hands, your voice, they've all been telling me the opposite. When you've touched me, when you've smiled at me—when you've walked beside me, when you've sat with me in the lounge. Whenever there are other people about, you've been happy to respond to me. But where we are alone——' He shook his head. 'I don't understand.'

But I do, Jan thought, staring at him with dismay. *Whenever there are other people about. . .* It wasn't quite like that. It was when *Marc* was about. That was when she'd responded to Kurt, that was when she'd given him encouragement. When she'd wanted to annoy Marc Tyrell.

'Kurt, I'm sorry,' she said in a low voice. 'You're right—I've behaved very badly. But it hasn't been quite as you think. And I do mean it when I say there's no future for us. I can't ever love you.' She lifted one shoulder helplessly. 'I can't say anything more than that. I'm sorry. Really sorry.'

He stared at her in silence. His face had hardened, grown grim. She stood very still, wondering what he was going to do, acutely aware of the remoteness of her turret room, of the fact that no other rooms were nearby, no one else within earshot.

'So it's true,' he said at last. 'What Marc Tyrell told me about you is true.'

'What Marc told you? What do you mean?'

'How often have you pretended to be in love with a man?' he went on as if she had never spoken. 'How often have you led him to believe that you returned his own passion—only to refuse him at the last moment?'

'Kurt, for heaven's sake!'

'How often?' he demanded implacably.

'*Never*! Kurt, what makes you think I would? Simply because——'

'Simply because you *have*,' he said gravely. 'Because ever since we met you have been offering yourself to me. Smiling your smile, touching my hand, letting me take your arm. Teasing me—coming close, laughing and then slipping away. Yes, you are exactly as Marc Tyrell warned me you would be.'

'*Marc*? What on earth does he have to do with. . .? Just what has he been telling you, Kurt?'

'Why, that you are the kind of woman you are. That you believe in equality of the sexes. No more than that— he did not need to say more.' In the growing light, she could see Kurt's face, grim and cold as she had never seen it before. 'I know what a liberated woman believes. She believes that women are better than men—superior. Ha! I've met such women before—yes, we have them here in Switzerland too. And shall I tell you how they end up? Not women at all—hard and arrogant. *Nothings*!'

'You mean Marc told you all that?' Jan breathed.

'No, merely that you are a feminist. The rest follows.'

She stared at him, at the handsome face, the dark eyes. The moonlight made shadows on his face and she saw for the first time that the sharp planes were already being blurred by conceit and arrogance. Slowly she began to see him as a man who, though careful always to treat women as something precious, to be handled with care and reverence, nevertheless would always see them as inferior beings. Second-class citizens. To be kept in their place.

'I think you'd better go, Kurt,' she said quietly.

He bowed ironically. 'I think so too. It seems we have both made a mistake.'

Jan watched him move away to the door and felt suddenly saddened. He had, after all, been generous and kind to both her and Marc. And he had been sincerely, according to his lights, in love with her. She hated to see him leave like this, bitter and angry.

He reached the door and opened it, and as he did so she crossed the floor quickly and laid her hand on his arm.

'Kurt, don't go like that. Say we can still be friends— please?'

He looked down at her, his expression unreadable.

'Yes, that's what they always say, isn't it—women like you? Well, and why not? You were honest enough at the last, after all. You did tell me there was nothing for us. And friendship is little enough to give a woman who has taught a man so much, so quickly.'

As she stood at the open door, dumbfounded, he bent and laid his lips on hers. His kiss was cool, passionless. He lifted his head, gave her one last look, and then turned away, leaving her trembling against the door-jamb, staring after him.

A small sound disturbed her. She turned her head and saw Marc Tyrell standing a few yards away, watching her gravely.

With a tiny, choking cry, she turned and stumbled back into her room.

CHAPTER NINE

'WHERE the hell,' Marc demanded through gritted teeth, 'is that video I took of the Falls?'

Jan, surrounded by notepads, typing paper, films, cameras and cassettes, looked up wearily. She had barely slept at all the night before and was finding just being in the same room as Marc difficult enough. Being in the same room with Marc in what was just about the worst temper she had ever seen him in was almost too difficult to bear.

'It was here with all the others yesterday,' she said, trying to keep back the tears that had been all too close ever since she had seen him outside her room last night. 'You must have moved it——'

'I certainly did not!' His voice was savage. 'I put everything together before I went to bed, ready to be handed over to Ken when we get back. Somebody's moved the damned thing.' He glared at her. 'And there's been nobody in here but us.'

'Well, *I* haven't touched it!' she flared, suddenly angry. 'I haven't been near your precious videotapes. You must have put it somewhere else. Are you sure you didn't——?'

'Look, I *told* you.' He gave her a withering look. 'I do happen to be aware of what I'm doing—unlike some people, who seem to be going around in some kind of a trance. And it doesn't take much to know what kind of trance either,' he added bitingly.

'And just what do you mean by that?'

'Oh, come on, Jan—don't take me for a fool. You know perfectly well I saw you last night—or should I say early this morning? It's obvious what was going on. A man doesn't come out of a girl's bedroom at that hour just because he's been reading the meter. Well, what you do in your own time is your affair, I suppose—literally. I just wish you wouldn't let it interfere with your work, that's all. That's the trouble with women, of course,' he added deliberately. 'Once their private lives start to get complicated, professionalism goes out of the window.'

Jan gasped. She felt her face whiten and stepped forward, fists clenched. 'Are you saying I'm not professional?'

His glance was like ice. 'When important items start disappearing, yes. And when you appear for work looking more as if you ought to be back in bed—alone, this time, for a few hours' sleep——'

Her arm swung of its own accord and her hand met his cheek with a sharp crack. Horrified by her own action, she stepped quickly back, but Marc caught her wrist and held it in a grip of iron. With his other hand, he touched the livid mark her palm had left. His eyes were blazing.

'You little hellcat! I'll teach you to hit me. . .' He jerked her towards him and Jan, caught off balance, stumbled and fell against him. Immediately his free arm came round her shoulders, holding her hard. She felt his fingers tangle in her soft curls, pulling her head back so that she was forced to meet his eyes.

Her heart kicked in sudden fear.

'Marc——'

'Yes, Jan?' he mocked her. 'What are you afraid of? That I'll hit you, as you hit me? I suppose that's just what I ought to do—in the interests of equality. After

all, you've told me often enough that you want to be
treated as a person rather than as a woman.' He looked
down into her eyes, his own narrow with anger, glimmering between half-closed lids. 'But do you know, I
find that I'm more old-fashioned than I thought. I
somehow still can't bring myself to start knocking
women about. Silly, isn't it? And, in any case, I've got a
feeling that it wouldn't be quite the right punishment for
you. No, I can think of something you'd hate much, *much*
much more. . .'

Jan stared at him and suddenly knew what he meant.
Panic-stricken, she struggled in his arms, but her efforts
served only to make Marc tighten his grip around her,
so that she was crushed against the hardness of his body,
almost unable to breathe. Helpless, she clutched him,
her fingers moving convulsively on his thin shirt. She
could feel the warmth of his body, the powerful contours
of his muscles, and a strange weakness flooded through
her so that she lay against him, her struggles ceasing.

'That's better,' he said harshly, and she lifted her head
and looked up at him, eyes mutely imploring. 'Now. . .'

There was nothing Jan could do about it. As her lips
parted for one last protest, his mouth took and possessed
them. She felt their warmth pulsing into her veins,
sending her blood singing through her body, and in spite
of the bruising savagery of the kiss her body responded
at once; she was on fire, melting, her bones softening
against him so that she was moulded to his shape,
helpless, yearning. . .willing. . .

In that moment she knew the truth. And knew a
hopelessness that brought tears springing to her eyes.

Marc's mouth left hers at last. The savage rage had
left him; his arms were still tight about her, but they
held her with tenderness now. He moved his lips slowly,

searchingly, with a passion that sought its own response, across her face, touching her eyelids, her ears, sweeping down her neck to the hollow of her throat. Jan's head fell back, exposing the arch to his mouth, and she moaned softly. How could she have deceived herself so? How could she ever have denied the love she felt for this man, this difficult, demanding man who wanted the best from her at all times, who would settle for nothing less, who fought and argued and scorned her, yet could take her in his arms and turn her to a quivering, whimpering jelly?

He was right—she ought to hate it. The kisses that were now at her breast ought to have her cringing in revulsion, humiliated and furious that he could over-power her by sheer brute strength, take her by nothing more than animal force. They ought to be punishment far more than mere violence.

But now, knowing at last the truth of her feelings for him—knowing at last why Kurt had never been able to arouse her, while Marc's slightest touch had sent fire scorching through her veins—she was helpless to do anything other than respond to him as a woman in love must respond. And when his mouth returned to hers, she met it with joy, with delight, letting her lips move against his, letting her tongue make its own exploration, touching, twining, tasting. Finding a sensuousness she had never known she possessed, she moved against him, delighting in the hardness of his muscles against her own softness, thrilling to the shape of him against her, as if their bodies fitted exactly, as if they had been made to be together and at some distant, long-past moment had been broken apart to live through a long separation awaiting this moment.

Marc took his mouth away at last. Jan felt him move

away slightly and she opened her eyes and looked up at him as if she had been drugged.

'Marc. . .' She whispered, then stopped, shocked by the look in his eyes.

'Hell, Jan,' he said slowly, 'just what kind of a woman are you?'

She stared at him. His eyes were dark, the pupils so wide that only a narrow rim of colour could be seen around them. His mouth, the mouth that only seconds ago had brought such delight, curled with what looked horribly like contempt.

'Marc. . .'

'Only last night you were with him,' he breathed. 'And now you behave as if there's never been another man in your life until this moment. As if you'd never——' He stopped, breathing hard. His nostrils dilated and she felt a kick of fear. She could feel the tension in him, the rippling anger that surged through his body so that he quivered against her. She shook her head, feeling the tears again in her eyes, and knowing that her true punishment was upon her now, worse than anything Marc could have devised.

'Marc, please—I wasn't—I didn't—it's not like you think——'

'Not like I think?' His voice, so dangerously quiet at first, rose as the words spat from his mouth. 'Just how is it, then? How else can it be, when you and he have been making up to each other since the first moment you met—when I've seen you holding his hand, gazing into his eyes like some moonstruck teenager, going off for solitary afternoons on that gin-palace of a motor yacht of his? When I've seen him coming out of your room after midnight? Don't take me for a complete fool, Jan,' he said with a bitterness that cut through to her soul.

'You've been leading him along ever since you first clapped eyes on him and his film-star looks—and certainly ever since you discovered just what a catch he would be!' He ignored her gasp and went on ruthlessly 'Not only a hotelier, but an aristocratic one at that— what hope would a poor TV director have with that sort of competition? But you still can't pass up the chance of a few minutes' idle dalliance, can you?' There was no mistaking the contempt now. 'You still can't say no to a bit of—of——'

'Marc, don't say it!' Her voice was agonised as she cut into his words, knowing that she could not bear to hear him cheapen the moments they had just shared. 'Marc, you must listen to me. Kurt and I—there's nothing—he doesn't make me feel as you do, I swear it—and we've never—even last night, we didn't—I told him I couldn't——Marc, please listen, please believe me——' The words refused to come in any sensible order; distressed, half crying, desperate to convince him, she knew she was making no sense. Already Marc was moving away from her; if she could not convince him now, she never would. She reached her hands towards him in a supplicating gesture, but to her dismay his glance flicked scorn at her and he turned away with a deliberation that tore at her heart.

'Don't go on, Jan. You're just making an exhibition of yourself. We both know the truth. All right, so Kurt doesn't get to you like I do. I might even believe that. But you're not going to let that stop you, are you? You'll still take him on—him and his string of hotels, his *Schloss* and his family name. Well, good luck to you— but don't imagine *I'm* going to be your bit on the side! You'll have to look elsewhere for your pleasures, I'm afraid—but be careful. Don't forget Kurt will be looking to you to provide him with an heir.' He wheeled and strode rapidly to the door. 'Meanwhile, don't forget you're still employed by 90s-TV, and I'm still your immediate boss—and find that damned video. I'm not going back without it!'

He jerked open the door, stormed through it and slammed it behind him with such a crash that the walls shook. And Jan, left alone in the middle of the room, stared after him with her hands at her face, white, shaking, and sick.

Time would prove to Marc that she wasn't going to marry Kurt. But what would convince him that she'd never intended to? And how could she ever expect him to believe that it was Marc himself that she loved—and always had, ever since that moment when they'd first met in his office with the little wooden otter at the window?

He wouldn't care anyway, she thought dejectedly, turning to look vaguely around the room. Not now that he'd met Renate.

The video was nowhere to be found. After searching for an hour, Jan was convinced that it was not in the room. Marc must have put it somewhere else and forgotten it— yet she dared not suggest such a possibility again. His reaction the first time had led them down a path she didn't think either of them wanted to tread again. In any case, further argument wouldn't alter the fact that it had been lost and that Marc blamed her for it—blamed her lack of professionalism.

That was what really stung. Whatever else happened between them, Jan had found comfort in the thought that he recognised her as a person who could do a job as well as the next man—or woman. The thought that, as well as everything else, she had now lost his professional esteem was something she couldn't tolerate. And didn't intend to.

So the video of the Falls had been lost. Well, couldn't another be made?

She glanced quickly at her watch. There were still two hours before they needed to depart. Time to drive into Meiringen and up to the top of the Falls. Time to do the necessary filming and be back before Marc—no doubt now wishing a tender and, probably, temporary farewell to Renate—had missed her. Time to hand him the videotape, even perhaps to run it through for him to see. Time to accept—graciously—his apology and retrieve a few shreds at least of her tattered self-esteem.

Marc might have the lowest opinion possible of her as a woman. But she was damned if she'd let him get away with calling her unprofessional!

The sun was hot on her bare head as she climbed out of the car at the top of the Reichenbach Falls and gathered her equipment together. She looked down at the foaming cascade that leapt beneath her, felt the spray cool on her face and took a deep breath.

The last time she had been up here was with Marc. They'd quarrelled that morning—as they had so many times—and Marc had challenged her, tried to make her face the attraction between them. He'd known then that the chemistry between them was too strong to be ignored, but Jan had stubbornly refused to admit it. Another man, she thought now, might have begged her—but not Marc. That wasn't his style. He'd want them to meet on equal terms—as two independent people who suddenly discovered themselves to be utterly dependent, after all, on each other.

But it wasn't like that, was it? Marc wasn't dependent on her at all. With him, it was simply a matter of chemistry—whereas for Jan, it was love. And commitment—a deeper commitment than she'd been prepared to give. That was why she'd refused so consistently, so *stupidly*, to face it.

Oh, but I'd face it now! she thought longingly. I'd commit myself now, if you wanted me, Marc. I'd commit myself completely.

But it was too late now. Marc would never believe that she hadn't preferred Kurt, with his glossy looks—what was it Marc had called him, a *knitting pattern*?—and his money, his hotel, his castle? And he didn't want her now, anyway. He wanted Renate.

With a sigh that seemed to drag itself all the way from the soles of her shoes, Jan lifted the video camera. Work, it seemed, was the only thing left to her.

She was halfway down the narrow, twisting path, her filming almost-finished, when she heard the shout from above.

'Jan! *Jan*! Where are you—where in God's name are you?'

Jan stood quite still, her heart thumping. It was Marc's voice, and it held a note she'd never heard before. A strange note, of anger edged with something else—fear? But that was ridiculous—what could Marc be frightened of? And how had he tracked her here?

'Jan! *Jan*!'

No, that wasn't fear. It was anger, pure and simple—rage because she'd eluded him, because she'd slipped out without telling him where she was going. As if she were a child, needing permission to leave the house. . .

'Jan! Answer me—for heaven's sake!'

Answer him? Just because he called? Why on earth should she? Why should she go running like a little dog when its master whistled? She hadn't asked him to follow her up here, had she? She was entitled to *some* free time, surely—time when she could go where she pleased and do as she liked, without the approval of her lord and master.

Quickly, Jan wheeled and set off down the path. She would go back to the bottom of the funicular and walk into the town from there. It would be easy enough to get a taxi back to the *Schloss*, and Marc could drive the car back when he got tired of yelling for her all over the mountain. By that time she'd be packed, rested and waiting for him, her emotions all neatly under control once more.

She heard him call again and smiled grimly. But at the next call, her smile faded. Wasn't his voice a little nearer? Was he coming down the path after her?

Oh, God! It was the obvious thing to do, after all—if she wasn't at the top, she must have come down the path and he would naturally follow her. She quickened her steps, ducking to avoid trailing branches, jumping over muddy patches, glancing over her shoulder. He couldn't catch her—she had a good start—but all the same. . .

'Jan! *Jan!* Please answer me——'

That edge in his voice again, almost of panic. She hesitated—was she perhaps behaving childishly, running away like this? But even as she paused, she heard his feet on the path above her, heard the crack of a branch and a muffled curse, and panic took hold of her too. She stumbled forward, rounded a bend in the path and came out at the brink of the tumbling stream, just below the main drop of the roaring fall, with thousands of gallons of water rushing away almost at her feet. The air was filled with spray, the bank slippery with mud. Jan saw it just too late. She tried to stop, but her foot skidded; she slid across the bank, her arms waving frantically as she tried to keep her balance. And then she fell, full-length in the oozing mud. The video camera flew out of her grasp, to disappear down the swirling torrent, and she slithered helplessly towards the edge of the bank, knowing that once she reached it nothing could save her from the bone-shattering descent down the rest of the cascade; and knowing that, unlike Sherlock Holmes, in her case there would be no resuscitation.

'*Jan*! Oh, lord——'

Marc's voice was as welcome as spring birdsong now, and his arms a strong and secure haven. She felt him catch her, stop her relentless sliding, drag her back through the mud; felt him bring her to rest on blessedly dry grass, looked up to see his face bending over her.

'Marc. . .' she whispered, and lifted her fingers to his cheek.

But there was no answering tenderness in his face. Instead, it was dark with anger and he jerked her roughly to her feet, glowering.

'You *stupid* little fool! Don't you realise what could have happened to you? You could have gone over those falls and been killed—or maybe that's what you intended me to think had happened? Was it? *Was it*? Because if so, I think it's just about the lowest, most despicable trick anyone can play—pretending suicide just to get attention and——'

'*Pretending suicide*? I wasn't doing any such thing!'

'So why did you come rushing out and leave the car there for me to find, if you weren't trying to frighten me rigid? What were you doing up here? Admiring the scenery? Grow up, Jan!'

'I think I have,' she said quietly. 'Quite a lot. And as it happens, you're nearly right. I did come to admire the scenery. Or, more importantly, to film it. I was remaking that tape you said you'd lost.' She looked round, realising suddenly that she no longer had the camera. 'Oh!'

'Well?' he said with biting sarcasm. 'What have you lost? The camera? Dropped it down the Falls, I suppose.' He caught her look of dismay and his jaw dropped. 'Jan, no! You haven't. . .'

'I—I think I have,' she said weakly. 'It must have flown out of my hand when I fell. Is it on the bank anywhere?'

But they both knew it wasn't. By now, it must have been smashed to pieces, all her careful filming lost. They were silent for a moment, thinking of what would have happened to her if she too had fallen into the raging water, and she gave an involuntary shiver.

'Well, it's not the end of the world,' she said a little shakily. 'We can still make the film again. You've got a spare camera, haven't you?'

'Yes, but no spare tapes. The others are all full——' Marc stopped suddenly and looked at her. 'Jan, which tape did you use? One you took off my table?'

'Yes, of course. There was a spare one——' She caught his look. 'It was spare, wasn't it? Number Ten—on top of the pile.'

'Number Ten,' Marc repeated expressionlessly. 'Yes, of course, it would be that one, wouldn't it? It would have to be.'

'Wasn't it spare?' she asked. 'I'm sure it was. There was nothing on it last night. I remember asking you, and you said it hadn't been used yet.'

'No more it had—then.' He drew a deep breath and gave her a strange look. 'But I used it after you'd gone to bed. I did an interview with an old man on the estate. He actually knew Conan Doyle—met him as a child and heard him talk about Holmes and Moriarty and the Reichenbach Falls. Renate arranged it and we went to see him very late.' His mouth twisted a little. 'That's why I was outside your room, incidentally—I was so full of it all, I just wanted to tell you about it. After I saw Brunner come out—well, it seemed to lose its thrill, somehow.'

Jan was silent. Slowly she looked down at her muddy clothes and tried to brush away some of the dirt. When she looked back at Marc her eyes were full of tears.

'I'm sorry, Marc. I didn't know—how could I? But you can do the interview again, can't you?'

'Not in this world,' Marc said without looking at her. 'Apparently the old man died soon after we left him last night—Renate told me just now. It's a pity—it would have been the central point of the whole programme. But, as you say, none of it was your fault.'

He turned and began to walk back up the path. Jan, feeling wet, dirty and dishevelled, followed him slowly. There had been a bitter sarcasm in his voice and she knew that there was nothing she could do or say to mend the rift that had opened up between them. It yawned at her feet: a dark, gaping abyss filled with mistakes and misunderstandings, and stretching across the rest of her life.

She understood now that for a short time she had had happiness within her grasp. And because she was her mother's daughter, she had failed to recognise it. And had thrown it away and lost it, as surely as the video camera had been lost in the Reichenbach Falls.

As surely as Conan Doyle had supposed Sherlock Holmes himself to have been lost in the same fearful torrent.

CHAPTER TEN

'TAKE you off the programme?' For once, Lucia paused in the act of lighting a cigarette and let it fall to the desk. 'Jan, you're not serious!'

'I was never more serious.' Jan sat tensely in her chair, hands clasped tightly between her knees. 'Lucia, I told you it would never work out—Marc Tyrell and me. We're like cat and dog. It's impossible. And it's going to get worse—so it's best to get out now, while there's still time to find another researcher.'

Lucia looked at her and shook her head. 'It must be working. The report Marc's sent me of the Swiss trip— between you, you've cooked up some really good ideas. And——'

'Lucia, *please*!' The ragged note in Jan's voice betrayed her tension. She took a deep breath, trying to control her voice, but it still shook a little as she said, 'If it comes to the crunch, Lucia, I won't ask you to release me—I'll just resign. That's how serious I am about this.'

'Resign? You mean from——'

'From 90s-TV, yes. I don't want to, but——'

Lucia looked at her again, her eyes narrowed, expression thoughtful. Then she shrugged and picked up the fallen cigarette.

'Well, if it's that important to you. . .I still think there's more in this than ordinary friction, though, Jan. You don't normally let things get you down like this. And I'd have said you had too much pride and self-respect to let a man get to you. But if you're deter-mined——'

'I am.'

The older woman sighed and reached for a large desk diary.

'Well, I can't force you to work with the man. I think it's a pity, all the same. A great pity. You two would make a fine team. All right, Jan, I'll put someone else on *The Great Detectives*. I've nothing else for you at the moment, I'm afraid. May be just as well—you could probably do with a rest. Why not take a break for a few days?'

'I might do.' Jan stood up. 'Thanks, Lucia. And— I'm sorry.'

'That's OK. We all get problems from time to time.' The producer watched her go to the door, her face still thoughtful. 'All the same, I'd like to know just what went on, over in Switzerland.'

But that was something Jan did not intend to tell anyone. Even her mother couldn't get the truth out of her, no matter how she tried. Eventually she gave up and decided to assume that Marc Tyrell was entirely to blame.

'I've always thought he looked a real hidebound reactionary,' she declared. 'You can tell by looking at those types—too good-looking for their own or anyone else's good. I suppose he thought you'd fall at his feet straight away and didn't like it when you didn't.'

Jan said nothing. Her emotions still confused and raw, she was having difficulty in disentangling the truth about Marc and what had happened in Switzerland. She only knew that it had been, for her, traumatic, and that she needed time to sort out her feelings.

'Typical of that sort of man, of course,' Susan Cartwright went on. 'All the same, I'm surprised you couldn't cope with him, Jan. I'd have thought that with your upbringing——'

'It's probably my upbringing that caused half the trouble!' Jan said suddenly, surprising herself almost as much as her parents. She looked at them, seeing them all at once through Marc's eyes—the strong, dominating mother, the father who would rather retire to his study and shut the door than find himself involved in any controversy. Yes, she thought with pity, he *did* look beaten. And tired. Older than he was. As if life had proved too much for him, as if his early struggles had worn him out and left nothing but a shell, a dry husk of a man in place of the vigorous youth he must once have been.

She turned back to her mother and saw there all the energy that had been drained from Professor Cartwright. The strong lines of the face, the positive set to the lips, the determination in the eyes. All admirable enough once—but when had they changed to hardness, to intolerance, to ruthlessness? And was she in danger of the same thing happening to her?

Marc Tyrell had thought so.

As happened all too often, Jan found her thoughts swinging away to Marc and to their last day together, the way she had left him with her heart full of unspoken regrets, unanswered questions. How had he felt when he'd learned that she had asked Lucia to take her off the series? Had he been relieved, thankful that the thorn had been removed from his side—or had he been sorry? Had she imagined that tenderness she'd sometimes fancied she had caught in his eyes, had felt in the few kisses they had shared—or had his savage anger towards her been a truer indication of his feelings?

If only things had been different, she had found herself

thinking longingly, if only we could have dissolved those barriers between us. And then she would scold herself. There could never have been any future for her and Marc Tyrell. They were too different. The undeniable attraction, the chemistry that had sparked between them—it had all been a cruel trick of nature, something that could only have brought about disaster.

And wasn't that just what it had done? In her heart, if nowhere else.

Her mother had recovered from her surprise and there was a dangerous note in her voice as she said, 'Your upbringing? What do you mean by that, Jan?'

'Why, exactly the same as you do,' Jan retorted. 'You should know—you've taken great trouble over the years to teach me about men. How they're always looking for ways to keep women down—keep us in our place. How there's never been a good one yet. How we have to be continually on our guard, continually fighting for our rights—by which you actually mean supremacy. Because you don't really believe in *equality* at all, do you, Mother? You want women to be top. You want to keep men down, just as they've kept us. No wonder I'm incapable of forming a real relationship with a man! You've destroyed all possibility of that.' All possibility of a relationship with Marc, she thought, and felt hopelessness flood through her.

Susan Cartwright stared at her daughter. Her face was tight with anger, her eyes snapping. 'Destroyed all possibility of your forming a real relationship? *I* don't believe in equality? Jan, I don't think you know what you're saying. That Swiss trip was obviously no good to you at all—it's brought you to the brink of a nervous collapse. I'll make an appointment for you to see a doctor I know, she'll——'

'No! I don't want to see any doctor—at least, not of your choosing.' Jan was trembling now. She could feel the bitterness of years, hitherto dormant and unsuspected, welling up inside her. Like a poisonous abscess, it had to be lanced, had to be let out. 'And I mean every word I say. Your so-called equality isn't equality at all. Equality means a *partnership*—working together, giving, taking. What you mean by equality is dominating. The not-so-benevolent autocracy.' She looked at her father, sitting at the table watching them both, and hesitated. What she wanted to say must hurt him—but it was hurting her more not to say it. Now that she had begun, she could not draw back. 'Look at your own marriage,' she said passionately. 'It's no marriage at all! You've become a tyrant, and Daddy's had no option but to close himself off. I suppose once upon a time he believed in women's equality and gave you your head—and you just ran amok—and now look, look what you've done!'

The two women both turned and stared at Professor Cartwright. Then Susan rose to her feet. Even taller than Jan, she was now majestic, and it took all Jan's strength not to shrink away from the anger in her eyes.

'Well, now that we know just where we are, it seems that there's no more to be said,' she said icily. 'Quite clearly, I'm to blame for everything that's gone wrong in your life, Jan. You, of course, are responsible for nothing. Just as your father had no choice in his own course. I'm only astonished that you don't blame me for all the ills of the world, while you're about it. You seem to imagine that I have enough influence.' Carefully, precisely, she placed her chair under the table. 'I have to go out now and address a meeting. No doubt I shall ruin a good many more lives in the process, but it's the only thing I know how to do.'

She turned and left the room. Jan watched her numbly. She had never spoken to her mother in such a way before and she was miserably aware that she had not made a good job of it now. Susan would never understand just what was in Jan's mind. It was the end of their relationship. And although she believed now that Marc had made her see the truth, she felt a cold loneliness at the thought.

'I'm afraid you've hurt your mother very much,' Professor Cartwright said, speaking for the first time.

Jan turned to him. 'Hurt her? I've made her angry, that's all. I don't suppose she'll ever forgive me for the things I've said.'

'Oh, she will—as soon as you forgive her for the things she's done.' He smiled. 'You don't really understand, do you, Jan? You're falling into the same trap as she did— letting bitterness distort your thinking. You see, your mother really is a fine woman. A little over-stretched now, I know—but she'll change and mellow, just as we all do in time. And she's still working out the bitterness of her own childhood.'

'Her own——?' Jan looked at him. She knew very little about her mother's family; they were all dead before she was born and Susan rarely spoke of them. 'Daddy, what do you mean?'

'Your grandparents had a very unhappy marriage,' her father told her soberly. 'John Manson was a violent man—he beat his wife regularly, kept her short of money, drank heavily and altogether made your grandmother's life and Susan's a misery. Is it any wonder that she grew up with a hatred of men? She saw us all as monsters.'

'But she married you. Because you're gentle and kind.'

'I try to be. And it's certainly my nature to keep out

of trouble. But you're wrong, you know, when you say we have no marriage. We do. We need each other and we give each other something that perhaps no one else could. And we love each other, Jan. Believe it or not, I love your mother—and she loves me.' He paused. 'You have to let people work out their own lives, Jan, my dear. It's taking your mother a long time to learn that, but she will. And so must you.'

Jan was silent for a while. Then she leaned across and gave him a kiss.

'Thank you, Daddy. I'll remember that.'

He nodded, smiling behind his spectacles. 'And what will you do now?'

Jan sighed. 'Lucia suggested that I should go away for a few days. Try to put the whole thing out of my mind and then start a new job as soon as she finds me one.'

'Any ideas where to go?' He turned and fumbled in a drawer. 'If you haven't, you might like to try this—a little village I know in Herefordshire. Quiet, peaceful— pretty countryside. You could do some walking— nothing like walking in the countryside for clearing the mind. I stayed there once a few years back.' He produced a piece of paper. 'Here—Knapp Farm, not far from Hay-on-Wye.'

Jan took it. 'Thanks, Daddy. It sounds just what I need. But I think I ought to stay here, for a while at any rate.' She gave him a lop-sided smile. 'What you've said about Mother has made me think. I haven't really been very fair to her. I'd like to—well, try to improve things between us.'

He nodded. 'I'd like that too. It's sad when a mother and daughter are at loggerheads. And you know, you two could be good friends, if you could only try to see each other's point of view.'

That was easier said than done, Jan thought over the next few days, as she and her mother struggled to find a new footing for their relationship. The things that had been said couldn't be easily forgotten. And much as Jan wanted to reach a new understanding, she wasn't prepared to compromise on the ideas and principles she was slowly beginning to work out for herself—ideas, she had to admit, that Marc had first introduced into her mind. Nor could she put the thought of him out of her head, nor the harrowing sense of loss she still felt every morning when she first woke from a night of tumbled dreams.

It was on the evening of the fourth uneasy day when her mother called her to the telephone.

'A call for you, Jan.' Her voice was toneless. 'I told him you were on holiday, but he didn't seem to understand.' She held the instrument out and Jan took it, supposing that it was someone from the studios, calling about some minor matter.

At the first sound of his voice, her heart lurched and her knees trembled. She sank on to a chair.

'Jan? Is that you?' His tone was abrupt, peremptory. 'Look, I've had hell's own job finding you. Why didn't you say you were going to be at home? I thought——'

'Thought what?' The familiar anger was already rising. 'Thought I was off on holiday in the Bahamas? Sunning myself in Morocco? Climbing a mountain in Iceland? Why *shouldn't* I be at home, Marc? And why should I have to tell you where I am anyway? I'm not working for you any more.'

'I know that,' he said grimly. 'That's why I've been trying to track you down. And Lucia's been no help— sent me way off course. Just what game are the two of you playing at?'

'We're not playing any games at all,' Jan said coldly. 'And it's nothing, repeat *nothing*, to do with you where I am. Now, if you've nothing more to say——'

'Nothing *more*?' The receiver quivered in her hand. 'Jan, I haven't even started yet! Look, there are a hundred things I want to know, and you've got to tell me. Starting with——'

'*Got* to tell you?' she broke in dangerously, but he swept on regardless.

'——why you ran out on me that way, just when we were getting some sort of a programme together. And why you——'

'I resigned because it was never going to work,' she cut in. 'You knew that as well as I did. But you just wanted——'

'——Kurt the way you did, fluttering your eyelashes and——'

'——everything your own way as usual. You wanted to fire me yourself—that would have given you great satisfaction, wouldn't it? And——'

'——looked as if he'd been cut off the back of a cornflake packet. Jan, he's not a real man, he's not for you. And anyway, he's tied up with——'

'——trouble with you is, you're just too arrogant to be true. You think every female you come across is going to just——'

'——your trouble is you just can't treat men as human beings, you think we're all after one——'

'——and if that's all you rang up to say,' Jan finished breathlessly, not having listened to a word, 'you might as well hang up now and save your money. *And* your breath,' she added, and took a deep, quivering one of her own.

There was a silence at the other end of the line. She

waited, and then began to wonder if he had done just that.

At last he spoke again. Quietly.

'Jan, it's no use going on like this. We can't talk over the phone. We need to meet. Look, I'm coming down to see you. Tomorrow morning, first thing. I'll be with you at ten, all right?'

He rang off, and Jan stared at the silent instrument in her hand; then, slowly, she replaced it on the wall.

Marc coming here? Tomorrow?

With a sudden surge of dismay, she knew she couldn't face him. Not yet. Perhaps not ever. She just wasn't ready for a confrontation.

She turned and ran up the stairs to her room, looking for the scrap of paper her father had given her.

Herefordshire. It sounded remote enough for anyone to lose themselves in. Marc Tyrell might come to the house, but he would never find her. Not in Herefordshire.

'. . .and if you really don't mind taking these eggs along, my dear, I'd be really grateful. I know they'll be needing them, what with all their family being here for the weekend.'

Jan smiled as her hostess produced a basket of eggs and handed it over. They were smooth and brown, some still warm from the nest. She felt a strange comfort in looking at them, letting her fingers stray over them.

'I feel like Little Red Riding Hood. I hope I won't meet any wolves in the forest!'

'Not many of them about here,' Mrs Harford said with a fat chuckle. 'But if you're not back by dark, I'll send out a woodcutter. Mind, they're a hospitable lot up at the Court, and you're as likely as not to find yourself stopping on for dinner. I don't know how she does it, the doctor—runs a busy practice and keeps a family going as well, though of course they're out in the world now, most of them. All the same, there's always someone staying there, and she never fails to have a grandchild or two about the place during the holidays. . .' Her cheerful voice rattled on as she saw Jan to the gate and pointed the way through the wood. Jan thanked her and set off, carrying the basket over her arm and feeling again absurdly like a figure in a fairy-tale.

She had been at Knapp Farm for almost a week now, and the tension was slowly draining away from her, leaving her more relaxed than she had been for a long time. Mrs Harford and her big farmer husband had been kindness itself; they remembered Professor Cartwright well, they said, such a pleasant man, and so interested in everything. He had helped with the harvest, been quite a useful worker too. Jan found difficulty in picturing her father as they saw him, and realised that what he had said was true—that you could never know all about another person's life. Certainly not about such a private and intimate part of life as a marriage. She realised that she had been as guilty as her mother of narrow thinking.

But she couldn't really blame her mother. Susan Cartwright, more than anyone else, had been insistent on independent thinking—the fact that she then tried to impose her own views on others was a typical quirk of human nature. She didn't have to be a saint.

Any more than anyone else, Jan thought. Any more than Kurt, forever searching for the ideal woman, yet almost snatching at excuses to see the feet of clay. Any more than Marc, demanding so much, yet prepared to give much, too.

Jan knew now that the chemistry between herself and

Marc, that powerful attraction against which she had fought because she'd been afraid it would subdue her, was more than just a physical response. There was something deeper between them—a bond so strong that it had refused to be denied. But her own headstrong refusal to be bound in any way had sent her running in the opposite direction—throwing herself into another man's arms, not because she loved him but because he was a protection. A protection against Marc, against the savage and tender kisses which had threatened to overwhelm her, against her own passionate nature.

What a fool she'd been! How blind, how reckless. And now she had thrown it all away—the only chance she had ever had of real happiness. Of a partnership in which both would be equal—arguing occasionally, yes, even fighting, but in the end finding a harmony that would bring deep peace to them both. A marriage in every sense.

Jan stopped in the little wood. She sat down on a fallen tree-trunk and set the basket with its cargo of eggs down in the grass at her feet. She put her elbows on her knees, bent her head into her hands, and wept.

Knapp Court stood on the edge of the wood, its back to the trees, looking out over the smoothly rolling Herefordshire fields. Beyond its cheerfully untidy garden, almost overgrown with rioting roses and a colourful jumble of flowering shrubs, grazed a herd of auburn-coated Hereford cows with their lord and master among them, white curls falling over his amiable brow. In the distance, Jan could see the blue shadows of the Welsh mountains.

She paused at the garden gate and gave her nose a final blow on her damp handkerchief. The storm of tears had taken her by surprise, and if she hadn't promised to deliver the eggs she would have gone straight back home. She was uncomfortably aware that her eyes must betray her weeping—but still, she reminded herself, she knew nobody at Knapp Court and needn't stay. She could just hand over the eggs at the kitchen door and leave.

It was very peaceful in the big garden. Somewhere she could hear the sound of children's voices and she remembered Mrs Harford's reference to grandchildren. But there was no one to be seen as she made her way to the back of the house, and she began to hope that she wouldn't even see anyone. Perhaps she would be able to just slip inside and leave the basket on the table. She really didn't feel like chatting now.

For a moment it looked as if her wish were to come true. The back door stood open and no one answered her knock. But as she hesitantly entered the big, cool room with its wooden cupboards lining the walls and set the basket on the big table in the middle, she heard someone singing. And before she could back away and slip outside, another door had opened and a woman came briskly in and stopped in surprise.

'Oh—hello.'

'Er—hello,' Jan said nervously, feeling as guilty as if she had been caught stealing the silver. 'I—I'm sorry to burst in, but Mrs Harford sent me over with some eggs and I couldn't make anyone hear.'

'Oh, that's because I was making so much noise myself,' the woman said cheerfully. 'The children always say we could be burgled and no one could hear a thing with the racket I make. I can't help it, you see,' she went on as she began to lift the eggs from the basket. 'It's frustrated ambition—I always wanted to be an opera singer.' She gave Jan a friendly smile. 'So you're staying with Mrs Harford, are you?'

'Just for a week or so,' said Jan, waiting for the last of the eggs to be removed so that she could retrieve the basket and leave. But the woman seemed in no hurry, and at the expectant expression on her face Jan felt compelled to go on. 'I'm just having a few days' break— a sort of holiday. Well, a rest, really.' She stopped abruptly, feeling herself in danger of saying too much. 'It's certainly a good place for a rest,' she added with a little, forced laugh.

'It certainly is,' the woman agreed. She looked at Jan thoughtfully. 'We haven't introduced ourselves. I'm the local doctor here—Dr Allen, strictly, but everyone calls me Dr Sue—comes of having lived here all my life, you see. Some of the older ones still find it a bit disconcerting to be attended by someone they remember seeing in her pram!'

Jan smiled. 'My name's Jan Cartwright.'

'Glad to meet you, Jan.' The doctor seemed to have forgotten that last box of eggs. 'Look, why not stay and have a cup of tea with me before you walk back—you did walk here, didn't you? Thought I didn't hear a car. . . The family's all around somewhere, taken the children for a picnic in the woods, I think, so we'll be nice and quiet for a bit. And that's something that doesn't happen too often in this house,' she added as she began to fill the kettle. 'Always someone around—my own fault, of course, for having five children, but I wouldn't have it any other way.'

'Five children?' Jan echoed. 'But however do you find time to—to——?'

'Be a doctor?' Sue Allen laughed. 'Oh, it's easy enough

if you're organised. That's the secret of being busy, you see—being organised. I wish a few more people would realise that.' She gave Jan a twinkling glance from bright grey eyes. 'Maybe we wouldn't hear so much nonsense about liberation then.'

'But surely——' Fascinated, Jan forgot her desire to escape and sat down at the kitchen table, her chin resting on her fists '—surely you *are* liberated? I mean, you're a doctor——'

'I have a career, is that it?' The kettle was full and plugged in, and the doctor turned and began to take delicately pretty bone china mugs from hooks on the dresser. 'Oh yes, I'm liberated—but only because I want to be. Because I've organised myself to be. Any woman could do that—she doesn't have to get permission from society, or even from her husband.' She laughed. 'People always assume you do, you know. "You must have a very good husband, Dr Allen—does he help with the housework?" As if it were entirely *my* job! I say no—he doesn't, because the housework *isn't* my job. It's *our* job. So we both do whatever happens to need doing. Always have.' She took an earthenware jug from the fridge and poured milk into the mugs. 'Quite honestly, I don't see any other way, if you both work. It's all a matter of common sense, really—if wallpapering is going to save money, let him do it and get on with the washing-up. And if it's the woman who's good at wallpapering, then *he* should do the washing-up and wash the nappies. Common sense!'

Jan watched her make the tea. It sounded incredibly simple—as the doctor said, common sense. Was it really so easy?

'But did you have any extra help?' she asked as the

mug, patterned with climbing roses, was set before her. 'With your housework and children?'

'Well, of course I did—I couldn't have managed without it. And I couldn't work full-time when they were babies—I had a part-time job at the local clinic then. And I still do all the cooking—I've always done that. Biscuit?' She produced a tin of biscuits that certainly looked deliciously home-made, and Jan accepted one. She was still thinking.

'But suppose it had come to a choice—your family or your career—what would you have done then?'

Sue Allen looked at her as if she'd asked how babies were born. 'Why, I'd have given it up, of course. But the fact that a mother goes on working full-time and employs a nanny doesn't mean she doesn't care. By the same token——' she leaned across the table '—the fact that a woman chooses to stay at home with her children doesn't mean she cares any more. She's simply doing what she prefers to do—and why on earth not? That's what being liberated means, my dear—doing what you prefer, while being adult enough to make sure that those you're responsible for don't suffer from it.' She poured more tea. 'My children learned to be self-sufficient, because I believed it was my duty to teach them to rely on themselves.' She gave Jan a sharp glance. 'Motherhood is a great responsibility, you know, as well as a great privilege.'

A privilege? Had Susan Cartwright ever seen it as a privilege? Jan had never heard her say so. But she shook herself—she'd already admitted that her mother didn't have to be a saint. And she'd done her best, according to her own lights.

That was something Marc hadn't understood, and Jan felt a sudden longing to talk to him, explain to him the new insights she had gained both from her father and from this warm-faced woman. She looked around the kitchen and wished she could bring him here, show him without words what her idea was of a real home. From the pale wood cupboard doors, glowing a soft gold in the afternoon light, through the gleam of copper and the shine of old china on the big Welsh dresser, to the bright pattern of the check tablecloth and the cheerful yellow of the milk jug, everything was warm and friendly. In the middle of the table was a bowl filled with summer flowers; in a corner stood an old chair, with a cat curled up asleep in the middle of a fat red cushion. But the real warmth came from this woman with her sympathetic face and her no-nonsense mind, and Jan wished again that she could bring Marc here, and introduce the two of them. Then maybe they could begin to make some sense out of the whole sad tangle.

'You know, you look very sad,' Sue Allen said gently, and touched her hand with light, cool fingers. 'I know we've only just met—but do you think you'd like to talk about it? Sometimes it helps to talk to a stranger.'

Jan gave her a crooked smile. 'I know. But somehow I don't feel you are a stranger.' She hesitated. Would it help to talk? Hadn't she gone over it all in her own mind until she was almost at screaming point? 'It's nothing much, really,' she said, wishing it were true. 'Just the usual thing, you know—man trouble. You must hear the same thing every day in your surgery.'

'I hear a great deal in my surgery,' Dr Allen said gravely. 'But I'd never call it "the usual thing". It isn't at all usual when you're the one it happens to. It's as new and painful as love is new and fresh—it happens for the first time to everyone, and it's just as real.' She smiled wryly. 'I've got it now in my own family—my son, who I never thought would be vulnerable, has come home like a whipped dog, covered with the bruises of some shattered romance.'

'He's lucky to have you to talk to,' said Jan, but the doctor laughed and shook her head.

'He hasn't said a word! He's not that sort—he doesn't dream that I even suspect. He forgets how well I know him. But of course, there's nothing I can say—not unless he chooses to bring the subject up himself.'

Before she could say anything else they heard voices in the garden and the kitchen door flew open to admit a tangle of children, none of them over ten years old and all talking at once in high, excited voices. Not even noticing Jan, they clustered around the doctor, thrusting untidy bunches of flowers at her, holding out stones and feathers for her inspection, patting any part of her they could reach, and generally clamouring for her attention. The noise was somewhat akin to that of a parrot-house at a zoo.

'Quiet!' the doctor shouted at last, holding up her hand, and they gradually fell silent. 'That's better. How do you expect me to hear you when you shout at me like a lot of untrained monkeys? Now, let's see what you've got. Alexis, that's a beautiful feather, do you know what bird it comes from? A pheasant? And what do you know about pheasants—not much. Go and find the bird book and look it up.' The small girl with black plaits scurried from the room. 'No, Jonathan, I don't think that's a fossil, just a stone. You ought to be able to see the shape of an animal or plant if it's a fossil—go and find Grandpa's book and see what it says. Peter and Anne, what have you got? Wild flowers—what a lovely bunch! You ought to be able to identify all those from my book. Why not bring it out here and we can look at them together? Lucy, you could be pouring some lemonade while they're doing that, I'm sure you're all dying of thirst.'

Lucy, tall and leggy, who had come in last, smiled at her grandmother and went to the fridge. Her eyes moved over Jan with a kind of grave interest, and Sue said, 'This is a friend who's staying at the Harfords' farm, Lucy. Jan Cartwright. We've been having a cup of tea and a chat. I hope she's going to stay for dinner too.' She looked enquiringly at Jan, who flushed with surprise. 'I was just going to ask you—we've been getting along so well, and it's so nice to see a new face. Good for the children too,' she added.

'Oh, but you've all your family here—Mrs Harford told me.' Mrs Harford had also said she was quite likely to find herself staying for dinner, but Jan hadn't taken her seriously. 'You can't want a stranger getting in your way.'

'You won't, and we can.' The doctor rose briskly to her feet. 'After all we've said about liberation, I wouldn't dream of trying to force you, but if you've nothing else to do this evening and would like an hour or two in a madhouse—well, you'll be very welcome. And I haven't *all* my family here—just a few of them. The children you've seen, two of my daughters and their husbands, and my son, who's deigned to honour us with his company for the weekend. And, as a matter of fact, that's all the more reason for you to stay.' Her grey eyes twinkled again. 'As you can see, the self-reliance I boast of having taught them is keeping them well and truly clear of the kitchen—and a dozen people is an awful lot to wash lettuce for!'

★ ★ ★

Washing lettuce was exactly what Jan found herself doing when the rest of the family arrived home.

By then she felt completely at home with the brisk, matter-of-fact doctor. Together they had sallied out into the sunlit garden to pick lettuce from the vegetable patch—'No, I don't do it all myself; old George Matcham from the village comes a couple of days a week, but I potter about whenever I get the chance'—and had stayed to gather strawberries, talking all the time. Sue Allen had been remarkably easy to talk to, warm and sympathetic without appearing to pry, and Jan had begun to wonder whether she might confide the full story of her disastrous trip to Switzerland. She felt sure that the older woman would understand; and, suddenly, she wanted very badly to have the kind of objective, common sense viewpoint that Sue Allen seemed to bring to everything.

Now wasn't the time, though, with the children running in and out and their parents expected at any moment. Perhaps later on. . .

'I should think that would be enough for even my hungry brood,' Sue said at last, looking at their brimming baskets. 'If you want an easy life, Jan, don't have five children! Although, on the other hand, there ought to be enough of them around to look after us in our old age. I wonder if anyone else has got back yet. My husband and son were off to Shrewsbury, to look at the abbey—you know, the one that's the scene of all those monk detective stories, set back in the twelfth century.'

Jan stared at her. 'Brother Cadfael. . .of course!' Why hadn't she thought of him before? One of the newest and most unusual of fictional detectives, carrying out his duties as a monastery herbalist in the long-ago reign of King Stephen and detecting ancient crime and murder along the way. . . She must tell Marc straight away! She felt a quick surge of excitement—and then the sharp stab of reality. Because there was no point in her telling Marc anything. Her work with him was over. They weren't even going to meet again. And as the thought formed in her mind, she turned her head hastily away to hide the sudden hot tears.

Sue Allen was watching her. 'Jan, are you all right? Has something upset you?'

'No.' Jan turned back, smiling as brightly as she knew how. 'No, I'm all right, it must be just the sun. . .' And then she met the doctor's straight, silver-grey gaze and shook her head ruefully. 'No, that's not true. But I can't impose my troubles on you—you're a busy woman, and your family——'

'That doesn't matter.' The grey eyes were direct and compassionate. 'Look, I can see there's something wrong. If you'd like someone to talk to—quite informally—come along and see me one day. Here, not at the surgery. Come and have lunch—I'm usually alone then. It often helps just to talk.'

To the right person, yes, Jan thought as she smiled her thanks. It hadn't helped much to talk to her own mother. . . She thought again of the contrast between the two women. Susan Cartwright, always straining for a situation that could never really come about. And Sue Allen—strange that they should have the same Christian name—who seemed to have got everything in balance, her career, her family. . .and all due, she would say in that brisk way, to common sense.

Was that really the secret? Was it really so simple after all?

Thoughtfully, Jan piled the lettuces by the sink and dropped their outer leaves into the bin. She began to strip the others apart and run them under the cold tap. Absorbed in this and in her thoughts, she was only dimly aware of the sound of more people arriving, of the children's voices as they clamoured for attention, each one determined to be first to show off the afternoon's treasures. She heard the light voices of women and the deeper ones of men. And then the deepest of all—a voice that struck at her soul, wrenching her away from her absorption, tearing her abruptly back to the present, to the here and now, to reality.

'Jan!'

Slowly, as if she had known all along that this must happen, as if it had been inevitable from the start, she turned from the sink and stared across the big, cool kitchen.

He was standing at the door. His eyes—grey, like the doctor's—glimmered in the dim light. He shook his head slowly, unbelievingly.

'Marc. . .'

CHAPTER ELEVEN

SUE ALLEN, coming back into the kitchen at that moment, saw at a glance that something had happened.

'Oh, there you are, Marc,' she began cheerfully, dumping a bowl of tomatoes on the big table. 'Just in time to give a hand with supper. He's the worst of the lot, this one,' she added, turning to Jan. 'Always conspicuous by his absence when there's work to be. . .' Her voice trailed away as her eyes moved over Jan's stricken face, and then she turned to the man who stood rock-still in the doorway. 'Have I said something? Do you two already know each other?' As soon as she had asked the question, comprehension dawned in her eyes— those silver-grey eyes, so like his. 'Oh. . .'

Marc moved at last. 'As you say, Mother,' he said grimly. 'Oh. . . Yes, we do know each other—in a way. And in another way——' his eyes were on Jan again '—hardly at all.'

There was a long pause. After that first incredulous glance, Jan had lowered her eyes, and now she stared fixedly at the lettuce leaves dripping in her hands. The silence was broken once again by Sue Allen.

'Look,' she said quietly, 'you obviously didn't expect to meet here, and it doesn't seem to be a particularly pleasant surprise. I suggest you decide quickly what you want to do before the others come rushing in. I invited you to stay for supper, Jan, and as my guest you're still very welcome. But if you'd rather just slip away——'

'Yes,' Jan said quickly, grabbing at the offer, 'I think

175

I would, if you don't mind. And—thanks for the tea and the talk and—and everything——' She dropped the lettuce in the bowl and wiped her hands hastily. 'I've really enjoyed meeting you, but I mustn't take up any more of your time.' Studiously avoiding Marc's eyes, she held out a trembling hand. 'I'll go this way, shall I? Oh, and if I could just have Mrs Harford's basket——'

Marc moved again, quickly, stepping forward to bar her way. 'Oh, no, you don't! You don't slip away from me again, Jan Cartwright. I want to talk to you.' His voice was hard, without a shred of tenderness, and she backed away, quivering. 'I'll come with you.' He lifted the basket from the table where she had put it and removed the eggs that still lay in the bottom. 'Did you say this is Mrs Harford's? You're staying there? Right— we can walk back through the wood.'

Red Riding Hood with the wolf. . .Jan stared speech-lessly at him, then turned in mute appeal to Sue Allen. But the doctor, watching them gravely, nodded her head.

'I think you should go with him, Jan. Whatever there is between you, it obviously needs talking about. And I'm sure you don't need to look so terrified—Marc won't hurt you. He's my son—he's been brought up to respect women.'

Marc gave a short laugh. 'I doubt if Jan can bring herself to believe that, just at the moment,' he said. 'She sees me as the original male chauvinist pig. I doubt if even you could persuade her otherwise about that. But you're right—we need to sort things out.' He turned and his silvery glance seared Jan's face. 'Ready, Jan?'

She hesitated for one more brief second, then capitu-lated. Marc was clearly determined, and she couldn't run away from him for the rest of her life. And after all, there was nothing he could actually *do* to her. His own mother was watching them go together. . .

'Yes,' she said in a low voice, 'I'm ready.'

'Right.' The voices of the rest of the family were coming nearer, a cheerful hubbub of conversation as they approached the kitchen. As Marc took her arm to draw her quickly out of the door, she felt the same familiar tingle and almost cried out at the force of it. At her gasp, he gave her a brief look and she thought his face softened momentarily. But then the sound of voices grew suddenly louder as the others came into the kitchen, and he jerked her round the corner of the house and out of sight.

'Over here.'

With rapid strides, he led her across the garden to a small gate in the fence. He held it open and Jan slipped through. Marc clicked the gate shut and indicated a narrow path winding through the trees.

'Come on. We'll go this way. It's all right,' he added impatiently, 'you can get back to the Harfords' farm this way. I'm not going to lead you deep into the woods and abandon you, like the Babes in the Wood.'

The afternoon seemed to have turned into a book of fairy-tales, Jan thought, and stifled a hysterical giggle. What would come next—Hansel and Gretel? Robin Hood? She felt Marc take her hand and shivered again, knowing that the hold he had on her was more than the touch of a hand. Would she ever be free of it?

The afternoon sun was lower now, but there were still several hours before dark. Marc walked quickly, his face set, his hand still firmly holding hers. Jan found herself almost scurrying to keep up. She searched among her churning emotions for indignation. How dared he drag her along like this? Just who did he think he was, anyway? And what could they possibly have to say to each other that hadn't already been said? But it was hard to whip up her anger, and after a few moments she gave up. She loved him; that was the trouble. And she'd rather have him angry with her than not have him at all.

Not that she would have him at all for very long. Presumably all he wanted now was to find out why she had left the programme so abruptly—though he must surely know that already—and subject her to one final harangue before they parted for good. She might have known he would find her somehow—Marc wasn't the man to let a woman have the last word. He would always want that particular pleasure for himself.

They stopped at last in a small clearing, where a large fallen tree lay beside the path. Marc brushed its broad trunk free of leaves and indicated that she should sit down.

'We might as well talk here as anywhere else. It's unlikely there'll be anyone to disturb us.'

Meekly, Jan sat down. She looked up at him, unaware of how defenceless and appealing her wide green eyes were, set in the ivory pallor of her face. Unable to fathom the sudden intensity of his gaze, she put up a hand and brushed back a stray red-gold curl. There was a quiver in her voice as she asked, 'Well, Marc? What do you want to say to me? What do we have to talk about that we haven't already discussed at—at length?'

'Quite a lot, I think,' he returned gravely, and sat down beside her. He took her hand as if to inspect it and she trembled as his fingers slowly explored hers, strong and brown against her own slenderness. In the trees above them she could hear a thrush singing; a soft breeze rustled the fresh green leaves.

After a few moments, Marc gave a little sigh. He

turned and looked directly into her face and Jan found that she could not drop her gaze. She was held there, mesmerised by eyes that shimmered like grey satin in the dappled sunlight. She felt her lips part slightly, knew that her heart was thundering against her ribs.

'Marc. . .'

'Don't say anything, Jan,' he said quietly. 'Not for a moment. Let's just sit here quietly, shall we? As we did when we watched the alpenglow together.'

Slowly she relaxed, feeling the tension slip away as she recalled the tender magic of those moments when they had sat at the window of the hotel in Mürren, watching the roseate glow of the sunset on the glimmering peaks of the mountains—the Eiger, the Monch, the Jungfrau. There had been something between them that evening, before they had really known Kurt, before Renate had come into their lives. Something precious. . .something that she had thought dead, never to be revived.

Was it possible? Was it possible that here, in this Herefordshire wood, the magic could be rekindled?

'Marc. . .' she whispered again, and lifted her face towards him.

But he did not kiss her. Instead he smiled a little and laid a finger on those parted lips.

'No, Jan. Not yet. We have to talk.'

'Talk?' she murmured. 'Why talk? Things always go wrong when we talk. We say the wrong things, we misunderstand. Don't let's talk, Marc.'

'But we must. To understand each other, we have to communicate. You of all people should know that.' His smile was faintly teasing now. 'Aren't you a media person? Don't you know the value of communication?'

She moved restlessly. 'But there are ways of communicating——'

'And we'll use them all. Believe me, we'll use them all. But first, we must talk.' His voice was tender but implacable, and Jan knew that there would be no further argument. Marc wanted to talk—and talk they would.

'I suppose you want me to explain why I walked out on the programme,' she said. 'I would have thought that was clear—we just couldn't go on working together, Marc. I couldn't stand any more of it—the arguing, the quarrelling. I felt—beaten, somehow. As if nothing I could do was right. And when I lost that camera and the film ——'

'I was furious,' he supplied as she hesitated. 'I agree, Jan, we'd got into a box—everything we did was on the wrong foot. But running away wasn't going to help that. And besides——' He looked at her with serious eyes '—Jan, do you have any idea what I felt like when I found you'd just taken off and nobody knew where you were?'

'My father knew.'

'I know.' He grinned. 'I went to see him—and even he wouldn't tell me. Said you needed time to think, to come to some conclusions of your own without being battered all the time by other people's opinions. We had a long talk, Jan, and he made me think too. I was wrong in what I said about him and your mother. There *is* something there—something valuable. It may not be the kind of relationship I understand, or could ever be part of myself, but there's love, and I was wrong to judge it as I did.' He paused. 'He made me see that, and he made me see that you did need time on your own, to think for yourself. I still think your mother was wrong to impose her own viewpoint on you—but I did the same thing. I tried to make you see things my way, and I shouldn't have. I should have relied on your own good sense.'

'But you were right,' Jan said. 'I was distorting

everything. And, having met your mother, I can see what you were trying to say. I understand it now.'

'There you are, then,' he said with a grin. 'Your good sense prevailed!' Then he grew serious again. 'I was wrong about something else, Jan. You and Kurt. I said some pretty unforgivable things there.'

'And I led you on to say them—I did my best to annoy you when Kurt was around. I behaved like a child,' she said honestly. 'And it got me into a very awkward situation. Marc, I was never attracted to him. And I'm not even sure now whether he was attracted to me. Thinking it over since—there was always something slightly artificial about the way he behaved. As if he were acting a part.'

'He was,' Marc said grimly. 'I don't know what he said to you, Jan, what promises he might have made you, and I don't think I want to. But Kurt never intended to marry you.'

He spoke so positively that Jan stared at him. 'How do you know?'

'Renate told me,' he said simply. Yes, Jan, I know what you thought about Renate, and I admit I didn't do too much to make you think otherwise—I guess it's the oldest game in the world and we all play it at times. And there were four of us playing it together at that *Schloss*. But there was nothing between me and Renate. There couldn't have been. For one thing, I was only interested in you. . .and for another, she was there simply to keep her eye on Kurt.'

'On *Kurt*?' For a moment, Jan let his other remark go. 'But—do you mean——?'

'Exactly. Renate means to marry Kurt—and I heard this morning that she's finally got him to name the day. They're planning a wedding in September and we're both invited!' He smiled. 'I think we might even go, don't you?'

Jan shook her head, bewildered. 'Marc, none of this makes sense. Are you telling me that Kurt and Renate were all the time——?'

'Kurt and Renate seem to have had quite a stormy courtship,' he said. 'Almost as stormy as ours. . . He could never quite accept that they should marry, you see—he held out against it. Had some idea that their cousinship was against it, for a start, although the relationship is really quite distant. And he was always looking for the "perfect" woman—who, as you and I both know, doesn't exist. Any more than the perfect man exists. . .hm?'

Jan caught the wicked glint in his eye and couldn't help smiling. She had relaxed in spite of herself, all her earlier fears dissolved. To her surprise, she found that Marc was sitting close to her, close enough to lean against.

'So they're getting married,' she said slowly. 'And you and Renate. . .?'

'I told you. Nothing.' His arm was around her, tightening to hold her close. 'I meant what I said, Jan,' he said quietly. 'I was interested only in you. It's been like that ever since I first saw you.'

She swallowed a little. 'I can't be one of your women, Marc——'

'*My women*? Jan darling, how often do I have to tell you—I don't *have* "women". I've had a few girlfriends and one serious relationship, that's all. And none of them have ever meant to me one tenth of what you mean.' His face was utterly serious now, his eyes as dark and soft as a dove's wing. 'I don't want you to be one of "my women", Jan—I want you to be my *woman*. My wife. Do you understand that?'

Her mind whirled. She stared at him, unable to speak. She shook her head slightly, unbelievingly. Her lips parted and at last he bent his head and laid his mouth upon them. And if his words had not convinced her, his kiss could not fail. With the touch of his lips, with their firm yet tender pressure, a pulsing warmth spread through her to lift her heart at last from the unhappy depths where it had dwelt so long, and she felt a soaring joy flood through her veins.

'Oh, Marc,' she said as he let her lips go, and her voice shook with tears. 'Oh. . .*Marc!*'

'Better now?' Marc asked at last, wiping her tear-soaked face with a large white handkerchief.

Jan nodded.

'How did you know I was here, Marc? Was it really a coincidence, your coming home this week?' It didn't seem to matter much—all that mattered was his arm, warm and strong around her shoulders, his body firm against hers. She closed her eyes and a last sigh shook her. Marc held her a little more tightly.

'Not quite coincidence, Jan. Your father wouldn't tell me where you were, but he did hint quite strongly that I ought to come home for a few days' holiday myself. So I suspected you might be somewhere in the area.' He grinned. 'I didn't expect to find you in my own mother's kitchen, though—that *did* come as a surprise! But he was right, you know—you had to come out of your shell and start working it all out on your own account.'

Jan nodded soberly. 'I know. And some of what you said was true, Marc—but it's all much more complicated

than that. I suppose everything is. There's no black and
white really, is there? Nothing's simple.'

'Not really,' he said, and his arm tightened. 'Except
one thing, Jan. The way I love you. That's simple—
clear enough for anyone to understand.' He bent his
head and she lifted her face for his kiss. It was deep and
tender, just as she had known it would be, and with a
promise of passion to come. But it wasn't the moment
for passion now, and she was glad that Marc had enough
sensitivity to realise that.

They sat quietly together for a long time, silent at
first, then, slowly, beginning to talk. Their talk ranged
wide and deep; by the end of it, what had happened to
them in Switzerland was open before them, like a book,
and there were no more secrets. And then, close and
warm, they were silent again.

'You'll come back to supper, won't you, Jan?' he
asked at last. 'I want you to meet my family. I want you
to meet my mother properly and know what a truly
liberated woman is like.'

'I already do. We spent the afternoon together.' Jan
frowned. 'Marc, I don't understand—your mother's Dr
Allen——'

'And Mrs Tyrell,' he said with a smile. 'She was
practising as a doctor before she married Dad, so she
kept to her maiden name. But she's very happy to be
known by her married name too—doesn't see anything
demeaning in it.' His arms tightened around her again.
'I hope you won't either, my darling,' he said softly. 'I
hope you'll be happy to be called Mrs Tyrell.'

She clung to him, suddenly needing his strength, his
reassurance, and felt the same leap of passion in his lips
as they tightened against hers. A tremor shook her and
she let her body melt against his. The world reeled about

her; she was conscious of birdsong in the trees, of a cuckoo calling somewhere. She found her lips released and she opened her eyes and looked mistily up into Marc's face.

Slowly, he drew her up from the tree-trunk and away from the path into a small, hidden clearing. The turf made a soft bed, the slender trunks of silver birches made a shimmering wall, their branches arching overhead, their leaves a tender green against the soft spring sky.

Marc laid her down gently on the springing turf, slid an arm under her shoulders and propped himself on one elbow beside her. His face was serious as his eyes, as grey as a hawk's back, searched her own. He lifted one hand, stroked a finger down her cheek, let it stray gently under her ear and down her neck. His hand came to rest gently on her breast, covering it, and she sighed with quiet contentment. For the moment, passion was again at bay, but it would return. Meanwhile there was this, and it was priceless, because only with the right person could come contentment.

'You know what's happened now, don't you, Jan?' he said at last, and she nodded. 'We love each other. We don't even have to say it, but we will, because the words are good to hear. We'll say it every day; and our hearts will say it every moment.'

Jan felt the tears warm in her eyes. How different from Kurt's romantic speeches—yet how much more sincere.

'But we're not going to be *too* liberated over this, are we?' he continued, and there was a smile in his voice. 'We'll do the old-fashioned thing—get married. Because I'm chauvinist enough to want to know you're mine, Jan.' His arm tightened under her shoulders. 'I want to possess you utterly, completely and forever. It's the only way for me.' She could feel his trembling, knew that he meant this with every fibre. 'All or nothing, Jan—so what do you say?'

'All or nothing,' she agreed shakily. 'I don't want to be your lover, Marc—I want to be your wife.'

'And I want both. But then I'm a man—and men are notoriously greedy. . .'

His lips were on hers again and Jan closed her eyes and gave herself up at last to the passion that now swept them both, untrammelled and free to take their bodies, their emotions and their minds by storm. She felt his hands on her breasts, on her waist, on her stomach and her thighs. She felt his lips on hers, on her cheeks, her ears, her neck, her breasts. He was calling up sensations she had never suspected, a thundering roar of emotion that almost frightened her. But there was no time for fear. Marc's own urgency had now taken over, carrying her along with it, and she felt a strength in her, a strength of passion that rose to meet and match his, a surge of desire that taught her all she needed to know to satisfy them both. All inhibitions had been tossed aside, all prejudice discarded. They were a man and a woman, no different from men and women down the ages, sharing the love that had lifted lovers to the heights since time began. Equality, liberation—these were just words. In love, they were equal, and so it would remain throughout their lives.

Little Red Riding Hood had met her wolf. And found that he was no wolf after all.

HARLEQUIN
Romance®

Coming Next Month

Available in February wherever paperback books are sold, or through
Harlequin Reader Service:

In the U.S.
901 Fuhrmann Blvd.
P.O. Box 1397
Buffalo, N.Y. 14240-1397

In Canada
P.O. Box 603
Fort Erie, Ontario
L2A 5X3

Coming soon
to an easy chair near you.

FIRST CLASS is Harlequin's armchair travel plan for the incurably romantic. You'll visit a different dreamy destination every month from January through December without ever packing a bag. No jet lag, no expensive air fares and *no* lost luggage. Just First Class Harlequin Romance reading, featuring exotic settings from Tasmania to Thailand, from Egypt to Australia, and more.

FIRST CLASS romantic excursions guaranteed! Start your world tour in January. Look for the special **FIRST CLASS** destination on selected Harlequin Romance titles—there's a new one every month.

NEXT DESTINATION:
THAILAND

 Harlequin Books

JTR2

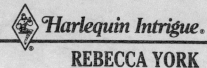

Harlequin Intrigue®

REBECCA YORK

Labeled a "true master of intrigue" by *Rave Reviews*, best-selling author Rebecca York makes her Harlequin Intrigue debut with an exciting suspenseful new series.

It looks like a charming old building near the renovated Baltimore waterfront, but inside 43 Light Street lurks danger . . . and romance.

Let Rebecca York introduce you to:

> *Abby Franklin*—a psychologist who risks everything to save a tough adventurer determined to find the truth about his sister's death. . . .
>
> *Jo O'Malley*—a private detective who finds herself matching wits with a serial killer who makes her his next target. . . .
>
> *Laura Roswell*—a lawyer whose inherited share in a development deal lands her in the middle of a murder. And she's the chief suspect. . . .

These are just a few of the occupants of 43 Light Street you'll meet in Harlequin Intrigue's new ongoing series. Don't miss any of the 43 LIGHT STREET books, beginning with #143 LIFE LINE.

And watch for future LIGHT STREET titles, including #155 SHATTERED VOWS (February 1991) and #167 WHISPERS IN THE NIGHT (August 1991).

HI-143-1

You'll flip . . . your pages won't!
Read paperbacks *hands-free* with

Book Mate • I

The perfect "mate" for all your romance paperbacks

Traveling • Vacationing • At Work • In Bed • Studying
• Cooking • Eating

Perfect size for all standard paperbacks, this wonderful invention makes reading a pure pleasure! Ingenious design holds paperback books OPEN and FLAT so even wind can't ruffle pages — leaves your hands free to do other things. Reinforced, wipe-clean vinyl-covered holder flexes to let you turn pages without undoing the strap...supports paperbacks so well, they have the strength of hardcovers!

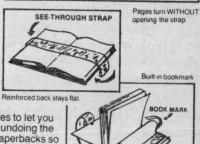

Pages turn WITHOUT opening the strap.

SEE-THROUGH STRAP

Reinforced back stays flat.

Built in bookmark

BOOK MARK

BACK COVER HOLDING STRIP

10˝ x 7¼˝, opened.
Snaps closed for easy carrying, too.

Available now. Send your name, address, and zip code, along with a check or money order for just $5.95 + .75¢ for delivery (for a total of $6.70) payable to Reader Service to:

Reader Service
Bookmate Offer
3010 Walden Avenue
P.O. Box 1396
Buffalo, N.Y. 14269-1396

Offer not available in Canada
*New York residents add appropriate sales tax.

BM-GR

HARLEQUIN
American Romance®
RELIVE THE MEMORIES....

From New York's immigrant experience to San Francisco's Great Quake of '06. From the western front of World War I to the Roaring Twenties. From the indomitable spirit of the thirties to the home front of the Fabulous Forties to the baby-boom fifties...A CENTURY OF AMERICAN ROMANCE takes you on a nostalgic journey.

From the turn of the century to the dawn of the year 2000, you'll revel in the romance of a time gone by and sneak a peek at romance in an exciting future.

Watch for all the CENTURY OF AMERICAN ROMANCE titles coming to you one per month over the next four months in Harlequin American Romance.

Don't miss a day of A CENTURY OF AMERICAN ROMANCE.

A CENTURY OF
AMERICAN ROMANCE
1960s

The women...the men...the passions...the memories...